A. E. VAN VOGT

THE BOOK OF
VAN VOGT

DAW BOOKS, INC.
DONALD A. WOLLHEIM, PUBLISHER

1301 Avenue of the Americas
New York, N. Y.   10019

CONTENTS

THE TIMED CLOCK

"MARRIAGE," Terry Maynard will say when he's feeling expansive, "is a sacred institution. I ought to know. I've been married twice, once back in 1905, and again in 1967. That kind of time interval gives a man perspective for a fair judgment."

And having said that, he looks blandly over at his wife Joan. She sighed on this particular evening, lit a cigarette, leaned back, and murmured, "Terry, you mad daredevil, you. Again?"

She sipped at her cocktail, looked with guileless blue eyes at the visitors, and said, "Terry is going to tell you the story of our romance. If you've heard it before, you'll find sandwiches and things in the dining room."

Two men and a woman got up and walked out. Terry called after them: "People laughed at the atomic bomb—till it dropped on them. One of these days, somebody is going to find I'm not just romancing. That what I say happened did happen and that it could happen to them. When I think of the deadly potentialities, the atomic bomb will look like a sputtering candle."

One of the men in the group that had remained said in a puzzled tone, "I don't get that. What can your being married in 1905 as well as now have to do with the A-bomb —entirely aside from the annoyance your charming wife may feel at not being able to sink those long fingernails of hers into the fair skin of her ancient rival?"

"Sir," said Terry, "you are speaking of my first wife—may she rest in peace."

"She never will," said Joan Maynard. "Not if I can help it."

But she settled herself comfortably. "Go on, Terry, darling," she said cozily.

"When I was ten years old," began her husband, "I used to be fascinated by the old grandfather clock in the hall—you can all look at it on your way out. One day, I opened the door at the bottom, and I was playing with the pendulum when I saw it was marked with numbers. They started near the top of the long bar, and the first number was 1840, and they went right down to the bottom, and the last number was 1970. That was in 1950, and I remember being surprised that the little indicator on the crystalline weight pointed exactly at 1950. I thought I had made a great discovery about how clocks worked. After I got over my excitement, I began, of course, to fool around with the weight, and I recall sliding it up to 1891.

"At that moment, I had a dizzy spell. I let go of the weight and sagged to the floor, feeling quite ill. When I looked up, there was a strange woman, and everything around me looked different. You understand, it was only a matter of furniture and rug arrangement. This house has been in our family for well over a hundred years.

"But at ten I was instantly scared, particularly when I saw this woman. She was about forty years old. She wore an old-fashioned, long skirt, her lips were pressed into a thin line of anger, and she held a switch in her hand. As I climbed shakily to my feet, she spoke: 'Joe Maynard, how many times have I told you to stay away from that clock?'

"Her calling me Joe froze me. I didn't know then that my grandfather's name was Joseph. Another thing that held me was her accent. Her English was quite precise; I can't describe it. The third thing that paralyzed me was that in a vague kind of way her face began to look familiar. It was the face of my great-grandmother, whose portrait hung in my father's study.

"*Swish!* The switch caught me on one leg. I dived past her and headed for the door, yowling. I heard her calling after me: 'Joe Maynard, you wait till your father comes home—'

"Outside, I was in fantasia, a primitive world in a small town in the late 1800s. A dog yipped after me. There were horses on the street, a wooden sidewalk. I had been brought up to dodge automobiles and ride on buses. I couldn't take the change. My mind is blank about the hours that went by. But it grew dark, and I sneaked back to the big house and peered through the only lighted window into the dining room. I saw a sight I'll never forget. My great-grandfather and great-grandmother sat at dinner with a boy my own age; and that boy was practically my living image except that he looked more frightened than I ever hope to be. Great-grandfather was speaking; I could hear him plainly through the glass, he was so angry:

" 'That settles it. Practically calling your own mother a liar. I'll take care of you after dinner.'

"I guessed Joe was getting it for me. But all that really mattered was that they were not in the hall near the clock. I sneaked into the house, trembling and without really having a plan. I tiptoed over to the clock, opened the clock case, and set the weight back to 1950. I did that without thinking. My mind was like a block of ice.

"The next thing I knew, a man was yelling at me. A familiar voice. When I looked around, it was my own dad. 'You young wretch,' he shouted, 'I thought I told you to stay away from that clock.'

"For once a licking was a relief. But I never as a boy went near the clock again. I did get to the point where I asked cautiously about my ancestors. Dad was very reticent. He'd get a faraway look in his eyes, and he'd say, 'I don't understand a lot of things about my childhood, son. I'll tell you about it someday.'

"He died suddenly of pneumonia when I was thirteen. It was a financial as well as emotional shock. Mother sold, among other things, the old grandfather clock; and we were thinking of transforming the old place into a rooming house, but a sudden industrial growth boomed the value of some land we had on the other side of town. I had been thinking about the old clock and about my experience, but what with college and then my stint in Vietnam—I was what you might call a glorified office boy with the rank of captain—I didn't get a chance to look for it till early 1966. I traced it through the dealer who had bought it from us,

9

and paid three times what we originally got for it, but of course it was worth it.

"The weight on the pendulum had slipped down to 1966. The coincidence of that startled me. But more important, under a panel at the bottom I found a treasure: my grandfather's diary.

"The first entry was dated May 18, 1904. Kneeling there, grandfather's diary in my hand, I naturally decided to make a test. Had my childhood experience been real, or had it been a delusion? I didn't think then of actually arriving on the same day as the diary date, but I set it for 1904 as a matter of course. As a last-moment precaution, I slipped a .38 automatic into my coat pocket and then grasped the crystal weight.

"It felt warm to the touch. I had the distinct feeling that it vibrated.

"I had no sense of nausea this time; and I was just about to give up, rather sheepishly, when I glanced around. The hall seat had been moved. The rugs were a darker variety. Old-fashioned drapes of heavy, dark velvet hung over the door.

"My heart pounded. I worried about what I would say if I were discovered. Nevertheless, after a moment I realized that the house was silent except for the ticking of the clock. I stood up and in spite of what my eyes were seeing did not quite believe that the miracle had happened again.

"I walked out into a town that had grown since I had seen it as a boy. But it was still early twentieth century. Cows in back yards. Chicken coops. In the near distance I could see open prairie. The real growth hadn't begun, and there was no sign of the city that would someday be. It could easily be 1904.

"In a haze of excitement, I walked along the wooden sidewalk. Twice, I passed people, a man, and then a woman. They looked at me in what I realize now was amazement, but I scarcely noticed them. It was not until two women approached me on the narrow sidewalk that I came out of my daze and realized that I was seeing flesh-and-blood people of the early 1900s.

"They wore ground-length skirts that rustled. The day was warm. But it had evidently rained earlier, for I saw mud at the bottom of their skirts.

"The older woman took one look at me and said, 'Why, Joseph Maynard, so you've come home in time for your poor mother's funeral. Where did you get those outlandish clothes?'

"The girl said nothing. She just looked at me.

"I was about to protest that I was not Joseph Maynard but realized it would be unwise to do so. Besides, I was remembering what the entry in grandfather's diary had been for May eighteenth:

> Met Mrs. Caldwell and her daughter Marietta on the street. She couldn't seem to get over my coming back for the funeral.

"I thought, slightly dazzled, slightly blank, *If this was Mrs. Caldwell and her daughter, and this was that meeting*, then—

"The woman was speaking. 'Joseph Maynard, I want you to meet my daughter Marietta. We were just speaking of the funeral, weren't we, dear?'

"The girl continued to look at me. 'Were we, mother?' she asked.

" 'Of course we were, don't you remember?' Mrs. Caldwell sounded flustered. She went on hastily. 'Marietta and I are all ready for the funeral tomorrow.'

"Marietta said calmly, 'I thought you'd made arrangements to go to the Jones' farm.'

" 'Marietta, how can you say such a thing? That's for the day after. If I've made any such arrangements, they'll have to be changed.' She seemed in control of herself again. She said sympathetically, 'We were always so friendly with your mother, Mr. Maynard, weren't we, Marietta?'

" '*I* always liked her,' said Marietta, with an ever so faint emphasis on the first-person pronoun.

" 'We'll see you then tomorrow at the church at two o'clock,' Mrs. Caldwell said quickly. 'Come along, Marietta, darling.'

"I drew back to let them pass, then walked around the block, back to the family home. I explored the house, half expecting to find a corpse, but evidently the body had been taken elsewhere.

"I began to feel badly. My own mother had died in 1963 when I was far off in Vietnam. And our family lawyer had

11

had to make the funeral arrangements. On many a hot night in the jungle I had pictured the silent house when she was ill. It seemed to me that this was about as close as I had gotten to the actuality. The parallel depressed me.

"I locked the door, wound the clock, reset the weight to 1966, and returned to the twentieth century.

"The somber atmosphere of death departed slowly, and I came back to a most worrying thought: Had Joseph Maynard really returned to his home town on May 18, 1904? And if not, to whom did the May nineteenth entry in grandfather's diary refer? The diary entry stated simply:

Attended funeral this afternoon and talked again to Marietta.

"Talked *again!* That's what it said. And since it was I who had talked to her the first time, was it also I who would attend the funeral?

"I spent the evening reading the diary, searching for a word or phrase that would indicate the situation was as I was beginning to see it. I did not find a single reference to time travel, but that seemed natural enough after I thought it over. Suppose the diary fell into the wrong hands.

"I reached the entry where Joseph Maynard and Marietta Caldwell made their engagement announcement. And a little later I came to the date under which was written, 'Married Marietta today!' At that point, perspiring, I put the diary aside.

"The question was, if it was I who had done that, then what had become of the real Joseph Maynard? Had the only son of my great-grandparents died on some American frontier, unknown to his fellow townsmen? From the beginning that seemed the most likely explanation.

"I went to the funeral. And there was no doubt about it. I was the only Maynard present, aside from my dead great-grandmother.

"Afterwards, I had a talk with the family lawyer, and I took formal possession of the property. I had him set up a trust for the land that fifty years later saved mother and me from having to become boarding-house keepers.

"Then I set to work to insure that my father would be born.

12

"Marietta was an amazingly difficult girl to marry for a man who *knew* that the marriage was a cinch. She had another suitor, a young fellow I could have strangled half a dozen times. He had a bubbling personality but no money. Her parents were down on him for that last, but it didn't seem to worry Marietta.

"In the end, because I couldn't afford to lose, I played the game unfairly. I went to Mrs. Caldwell and told her bluntly that I wanted her to start encouraging Marietta to marry this other guy and to start criticizing me. I suggested that she point out that I was not reliable and that at any time I was apt to go wandering off to some far corner of the world, taking her with me to heaven only knew what hardships.

"As I had begun to suspect, that little girl had an adventurous streak in her. I don't know just how much her mother was able to reverse her attitude, but suddenly Marietta was more friendly. I had become so intent on the courtship that I'd kind of forgotten about the diary. After we became engaged, I looked it up, and there it was written up exactly for the day it happened.

"That gave me a grisly feeling. And when Marietta set the wedding day for the date given in the diary, I came even further out of my fantasy and in the most serious fashion considered my position. If I went through with this thing, then I would be my own grandfather. If I didn't go through with it, then what?

"Thinking about it just made me feel blank. But I looked around for a duplicate to the ancient leather diary, copied the old one word for word, and put the new one under the panel in the bottom of the clock. I suppose they were actually the same diary since the one I put in there must be the one I later found.

"Marietta and I were married as scheduled, and it wasn't long before we were able to guess that my father would be born in due course—though, naturally, Marietta didn't think of it in that way."

His account was interrupted. A woman said acidly, "Are we to understand, Mr. Maynard, that you actually went through with the marriage and that that poor girl is *now* going to have a baby?"

Maynard said mildly, "All this happened back in the early 1900s."

The woman's color was high. "I think this is the most outrageous thing I have ever heard."

Maynard gazed quizzically at his audience. "How do the rest of you feel about this? Do you feel that a man hasn't the moral right to insure that he be born?"

"Well—" a man began doubtfully.

Maynard said, "Don't you think I'd better finish the story before we talk?"

"My troubles," he went on, "began almost immediately. Marietta wanted to know where I went to when I disappeared. She was damnably inquisitive about my past. Where had I been? What places had I visited? What made me leave home in the first place? Since I was not Joseph Maynard it wasn't long before I felt like a hen-pecked husband. I had intended to stick with her at least until the baby was born, with only occasional journeys to the twentieth century. But she followed me around the house. Twice, she almost caught me using the clock. I grew alarmed; then I realized that Joseph Maynard would have to vanish again from his age, this time forever.

"After all, what would be the point in my insuring my eventual birth if that was all I succeeded in doing? I had a life to live in 1967 and afterwards. There was even the problem of getting married again and having children who would carry on the line into the future.

"In the end I made the break. There was nothing else to do."

For a second time he was interrupted. "*Mister* Maynard," said the same woman who had previously spoken, "do you mean to sit there and tell us that you deserted that poor girl and her unborn baby?"

Maynard spread his hands helplessly. "What else? After all, she was well looked after. I even told myself that she might eventually marry the bubbling young man—though quite frankly I didn't like the idea."

"Why didn't you bring her up here?"

"Because," said Terry Maynard, "I wanted the baby back *there*."

The woman was white-faced and so angry that she stammered. "Mr. Maynard, I don't know whether I care to remain any longer under your roof."

Maynard was astonished. "Madam, do you *believe* this story?"

She blinked at that and said, "Oh!" Then she leaned back and laughed in an embarrassed fashion. Several people laughed at her, uncertainly.

Maynard went on. "You can't imagine how guilty I felt. Every time I looked at a pretty girl the specter of Marietta would rise up before me. And I had a hard time convincing myself that she probably died somewhere in the 1940s or even earlier. And yet, after only four months, I couldn't clearly remember what she looked like.

"Then one night at a party I met Joan. She reminded me instantly of Marietta. And that was all I needed, I guess. I have to admit that she was the aggressor in the courtship. I was glad of that, however, as I'm not sure I would have taken the plunge if there hadn't been someone like Joan pushing at me.

"We were married, and as is the custom I carried her across the threshold of the old house. After I had set her down, she stood looking at me for a long time with the oddest expression on her face. At last she said in a low voice, 'Terry, I have a confession to make.'

" 'Yes?' I couldn't imagine what it might be.

" 'Terry, there's a reason why I rushed you into this marriage.'

"That gave me a sinking sensation. I had heard of girls marrying hastily for certain reasons.

" 'Terry, I'm going to have a baby.'

"Having said that, she came over and slapped me in the face. I don't think I've ever been more bewildered in my life."

He paused, and looked around the room. People were staring at each other uncomfortably. Finally, the woman who had already been critical said with satisfaction, "Served you right."

"You think I deserved a deal like that?"

"Anybody," began the woman, "who will pull the kind of stunt—"

"But, look, madam," Maynard protested, "I discovered that unless I became my own grandfather, I would never be born. What would you have done in my position?"

"Sounds like bigamy to me," said a man. "Understand, I don't condone any woman trying to saddle a man with her illegitimate child. Joan, I'm surprised at you." He was an old friend of the Maynards who was hearing the story for the first time.

Joan murmured, "A woman can get just so desperate."

Maynard said, "Is it bigamy if the first wife has presumably been dead for a generation?" He broke off. "Besides, I had to think of the whole human race."

"What do you mean?" Several people spoke simultaneously.

"Try," was the earnest answer, "to imagine the forces that are at work in this time-travel process. I'm no scientist, but I have a picture of the whole world of matter moving through time according to an orderly law of energy.

"Beside that force, the atomic bomb can't be more than a faint flicker of light in endless darkness. Suppose at a certain moment in the grand progression of space-time, a baby would fail to appear where a baby should have been. Since this particular baby grew up to be my father, if he, as the original baby, had not been born, would he and I continue to exist? And if we didn't, would our sudden disappearance affect the rest of the universe?"

Maynard leaned forward and said solemnly, "I think it would affect everything else. I think the entire universe would simply have vanished—poof!—gone instantly as if it had never been. The balance of life and existence must be immeasurably delicate. Put a strain on it, break the weakest link, and the whole structure crumbles. Could I, suspecting that possibility, have done other than I did?"

He shrugged, spread his hands questioningly, and leaned back.

There was silence. Then a man said, "Well, it looks to me as if you both got what you deserved." He frowned at Joan. "I've known you spasmodically for three years, and I don't recall any baby. Did it die, and if so, why bring out the family wash and hang it out in the front yard?"

Maynard said, "Joan, you'd better finish this story."

His wife glanced at her watch. "Do you think there's time, dear? It's twenty minutes to midnight. People like to celebrate the New Year."

"You can make it brief," said Maynard.

Joan said, "Actually, Terry's fear that his inquisitive Marietta would see him go into the future or come back from it was justified. As it happened, she saw him disappear. If you'll think that over, you'll realize that it had to take place that way. If she had seen him come back, she would in her hysteria have confronted him. As it was, she had time for a period of terrible turmoil and then for gradual recovery.

"No wonder she followed him around like a nervous hen. She had a burden of unspoken words to pour forth, but she dared not speak them. Several times, then, she saw him come and leave. The experience became less terrifying with repetition; and finally she grew curious. One day, when he got up before she awakened, leaving a note on his pillow to the effect that he would be gone for two days, she dressed for travel, taking with her all the money in the house, and went down to the clock. She had previously examined it and formed a theory as to how it operated. She saw that once more it was set for 1967.

"She grasped the crystal as she had seen her husband do; and presently she had a moment of nausea. Although she didn't know it immediately, she was in the twentieth century. Outside, she found herself in a nightmare. As she started to cross the street, a mechanical monster rushed at her, and there was a squeal as it came to a stop. An angry man leaned out of a window and berated her.

"Trembling, almost on the verge of fainting, she reached the sidewalk. She grew more cautious, and she learned quickly. In less than half an hour, she came to a store with dresses in the window. She went inside, took out her money, and asked the salesgirl who came up if it was any good. The girl called the manager. The manager sent one of the bills over to the nearby bank and had it checked.

"Marietta bought a dress, a suit, underclothing, accessories, and shoes. She went out of that shop, trembling at her temerity in wearing such shameless clothing but very determined. She was tired now, so she returned to the house and went back to her own age.

"As the days went by, she grew more daring. She was suspicious of her husband's intentions; and she had no standards by which to judge how far those twentieth-century hussies leaned in the direction of being modern. She learned to smoke, though it nearly choked her at first. She learned to drink, although after her first drink she slept for an hour, out like a light. She got herself a job in a store—they thought she had an old-fashioned accent that would please their customers. They fired her in less than a month, principally because she imitated the slangiest girls in the place but partly because she didn't always turn up for work.

"She was pretty sure by now that she was going to have her baby. And since at that time her husband hadn't left her permanently, she told him. I think she hoped he would take her into his confidence. I'm not sure of all that. It's hard to tell all about a woman's—or a man's—motives. Anyway, it didn't work. Presently, he went away and didn't come back.

"Guessing what he planned, she was furious. And yet there was a conflict going on inside her. On the one hand, she was the woman scorned. On the other, she was the woman who might be able to do something about what had happened.

"She closed up the house. She announced she was going away on a trip. Arrived in 1967, she got herself a job and rented a room under the maiden name of her mother, Joan Craig. She got herself invited to a party at which she met Terry Maynard. With her new hairdo and clothes, she resembled the original Marietta only vaguely.

"She married the guy and as punishment for what he had intended to do to her, gave him one of the big shocks of his life. And then, well, what could she do? When a man marries a girl twice, the second time without knowing who she is, it must be love—my goodness, it's three minutes to midnight. I've got to go and feed the toddler."

She leaped to her feet and disappeared into the hall.

When she had gone about a minute, a man broke the silence: "Well, I'll be hanged. So not only are you your own grandfather, but you're married in 1970 to your grandmother. Doesn't that make things a little complicated?"

Maynard shook his head. "It's the only solution, don't you see? We have one child—back there. He becomes my father. Any other children that are born we keep up here to carry on. It makes me feel a lot easier."

Far away, whistles began to blow. Maynard raised his glass. "Ladies and gentlemen, to the future—to 1971 and all that may follow."

When they had drunk, a woman said diffidently, "Did your wife—Joan—go back just now?"

Maynard nodded.

"What I don't understand," she went on, "is, you said the figures on the pendulum of the clock went to 1970. Well, 1970 just ended."

"Huh!" said Terry Maynard. A startled look came into his face. He half rose from his seat, almost spilling his cocktail. Slowly, he sank back again. He mumbled, "I'm sure it'll be all right. Fate couldn't be that ironic."

The woman who had been so critical earlier climbed to her feet. Her lips were drawn into a thin line. "Mr. Maynard, aren't you going to go and see?"

"No, no, it's all right, I'm sure. There's space for more numbers under the weight. It'll be just a matter of carving more numbers. I feel very sure of that."

A man walked with deliberate strides to the hall door. He came back frowning. "You will be interested to know," he said, "that your clock has stopped—exactly on the hour of midnight."

Maynard stayed where he was. "I'm sure it'll be all right," he muttered.

Two women stood up. "We're going upstairs to look for Joan," said one.

They came back presently. "She's not there. There's no sign of her."

The two men and the woman who had gone into the dining room when Maynard first started his story emerged. One of the men said cheerfully, "It's after midnight, so I imagine it's all over." He glanced at Maynard. "Did you tell them the numbers ended at 1970?"

The guests stirred from their strained silence. The man addressed them in the same cheerful tone. "When I heard it, it was 1968—and exactly on the dot of midnight the clock stopped."

Somebody said, "Had Joan disappeared about three minutes before?"

"Yep."

Several guests went out into the hall to look at the clock. Words drifted back: ". . . By golly, it does end at 1970 . . . Wonder if Maynard has a new number carved in each year . . . Hey, Pete, grab the weight. . . . Not me, I feel just a little uneasy about that story . . . Maynard always was an odd fellow . . . Told it well, didn't he? . . ."

Later, as the guests were leaving, a woman said plaintively, "But if it was just a joke, why didn't Joan come back?"

A disembodied voice sounded from the darkness beyond the door. ". . . The Maynards are such an interesting couple, aren't they? . . ."

THE CONFESSION

MARRIOTT AWAKENED, remembering the impossible thing he had seen the night before in the empty living room. The memory, sharp and clear as a visual image, brought him out of bed with a jerk. He slipped into his dressing gown, and he was on his way to the living room when he slowed and stopped, thinking, *This is silly. It was only a dream.*

He shook his head, smiling reproachfully at himself. His bedroom had formerly been the storeroom of the old Marriott place. He had chosen it without regard for beauty because it adjoined the kitchen and could be heated by the kitchen stove. He turned into the kitchen now, briskly, rekindled the fire, heated water, washed, shaved, and dressed. He recalled with a smile how once, more than a year before, he had leaped madly out of bed and snatched the receiver off the phone—only to realize that it hadn't rung at all.

He put on his topcoat and paused to survey himself in the hall mirror. It was a faded mirror, and the image he saw was blurred. But what there was of it showed him a young man, thirtyish, slim of build and wearing a gray hat and topcoat. Satisfied, he permitted his eyes to stray to one side so that briefly the great hall was in his line of vision. The emptiness as always gave him a tiny yet palpable shock. What disturbed him most, however, was the realization that his gaze had shifted automatically to the living-room door. Marriott's lips curled.

"You damned fool," he said angrily to the image in the

mirror. "What are you trying to do? Prove yourself an idiot?"

He felt quite pleased that the living-room door was shut. Deliberately, he averted his gaze and opened the front door. A cold April wind buffeted his face. He locked the door behind him and walked to the front gate. It creaked as he opened it, but the rusty hinges had long since ceased to bother him. He closed the gate, and then as was his habit he paused for a look toward the end of the street.

The street was a long one, and the more distant houses straggled so deceptively that it was almost impossible to decide where the open country began. Paul Marriott sighed. His father had told him, not once but many times, that at the turn of the century the Marriott place had been nearly a quarter of a mile beyond the periphery of Hampden, a geometrically beautiful house with twenty acres of wooded estate, the showplace of the village. Gradually, it moved into the developing town until now it was inside the business section of the city.

It took Marriott three minutes to reach Aunt Mary's Breakfast Nook. He settled himself, and when the waitress came up, asked, "Judith come in yet?"

The girl shook her head with a faint frown, hesitated, and then said, "Now, honey, you know very well Miss Judith doesn't eat here anymore."

Marriott smiled, but he was annoyed with himself. He had asked about Judith because, well, he couldn't decide just why. The waitress changed the subject.

"How do you feel after the show last night?"

"Fine."

The girl marveled. "He sure had you prancing around the stage." She giggled. "For a minute I thought he was going to make you take off your pants."

Marriott smiled, more vaguely this time, and gave his order. He sat somber after she had gone, picturing the spectacle of the last survivor of the Marriott family making a spectacle of himself before an audience that, he had discovered, appreciated the decline of the Marriott fortune more than he did. He had been reluctant to go up, but there was a vociferous group of young men who had insisted. His breakfast was being served when one of the men entered the café and waved at Marriott, who waved back cheerfully and said, "Hi, Greg."

The big young man grunted as he eased himself into the booth across from Marriott. He boomed his order at the waitress, then turned to Marriott.

"The human nervous system is sure a funny thing, isn't it?"

Marriott nodded.

"Did you," Greg persisted, "really see that little puppy you pretended to be patting?"

Marriott shrugged. "I don't remember."

"Nothing at all?" In surprise.

"I have a vague memory of Blandar asking me to look into his right eye, and then he stroked my hands—I think."

"That's right. And he explained to you that one out of five people could go deep the first time."

"I guess I was one of those," said Marriott.

He was anxious to leave now. He gulped down his coffee and mumbled something about being late for work. He reached Clayton's Men's Wear at five to nine, unlocked the door, and began to sweep up. At ten minutes after nine young Pete Clayton arrived, and then several farmers came in. At nine-thirty old Pete Clayton stamped through to the office at the back and remained there all morning examining the books. His absence relieved Marriott; he was worried about Judith, and he didn't want to have the pressure of old Pete's presence to disturb him. Not, he told himself, that he liked worrying. Still, it was important to think things over at times.

What, he wondered, frowning, *did the waitress at Aunt Mary's Breakfast Nook mean when she said that I knew Judith didn't eat there anymore?* It hadn't struck him before that he didn't know why. He felt himself on the edge of a discovery. Just before eleven, ignoring the frown of the younger Clayton, he took off a minute to call up Judith at the bookstore. Her father answered, and Marriott was amazed when his question was answered by a dead silence, and then, "Uh, is that you, Paul?"

"Yes, Mr. Garson. Funny thing is I've been worried about her all morning and—is she out?"

Silence; finally, "Look, Paul, how about you coming over to the bookstore? I'd like to have a talk with you."

23

The older man's voice sounded quite serious. Paul shrugged and said, "Why, sure, sir. I'll drop by during my lunch hour."

His mind was singularly blank the rest of the morning. He ate lunch without appetite, feeling unexpectedly exhausted. *I must have worked harder this morning than I realized,* he decided.

All afternoon the store swarmed with farmers. Marriott ate his dinner with a better appetite and went to a show to relax. It was not until he was climbing the steps of the house around ten o'clock that he remembered that he hadn't gone to see Mr. Garson.

"I'll have to make a point of seeing him tomorrow," he told himself.

Inside, he turned on the hall light and casually glanced at the living-room door. Instantly his mind leaped to a memory of what he had seen the night before. Marriott shook himself angrily. It was really time he had a look in that room.

The living room was the same as it had been the previous night. For more than four years it had been as empty as the rest of the main part of the house. Now, it was completely furnished. A middle-aged man and a middle-aged woman sat motionless in chairs at opposite sides of the room. The woman was holding a book; the man simply sat. For the full minute that Marriott stood there glaring at them they did not move a finger or look at him. Finally, not knowing what else to do, Marriott closed the door and retreated into the kitchen.

He rekindled the fire, undressed, and crawled into bed. He told himself that he ought to call the police, but he had a curious sense of having seen the people in the room before. If he didn't know better, he would have identified the woman as Judith as she would be at forty-five. As for the man—

Long after midnight, Marriott awakened with a start, realizing that he had fallen asleep in the middle of a thought, the thought that the man bore an astonishing resemblance to himself as he might be twenty years hence.

He climbed out of bed, turned on the lights, and went to the living room. He half expected to find the scene gone, but it was still there, unchanged, the man and woman occupying exactly the same positions that they had earlier. What was different was his own feeling. Very simply, without fear, he knew that he had to go in and look at the two people.

Unhesitatingly, he stepped across the threshold.

Marriott stirred in his chair and glanced at Judith. He had a curious memory of having come into the room that minute, but he knew that he had been sitting beside the window for nearly an hour. He started to dismiss the thought when the unusualness of it penetrated anew.

"Well, I'll be damned," he said aloud, explosively.

Judith looked up from her book. "What's the matter, darling?"

Marriott hesitated. The remembrance in his mind was beginning to disturb him, and he thought of it suddenly as a private affair.

"Oh, nothing," he mumbled. "I think I'll go for a walk before bedtime—as far as the shop," he added. "See if everything is all right."

Judith seemed to accept the explanation and the purpose as normal, for she returned to her book. Marriott went out into the hall, put on his hat, and then paused before the mirror. The image that stared back at him was that of a dapper man of fifty. He found the sight more interesting than usual because he studied himself with an intentness that abruptly startled his mind.

What the hell, he thought, *an old fellow like me looking for beauty.*

Outside, he was amazed to realize he was perspiring. It was a warm night, so he wiped the wetness from his face with his handkerchief and shook his head wonderingly. *Am I going to be sick?* But he walked to the gate without any sense of nausea and more alive to his surroundings than he had been in many years. The old Marriott place was really deep inside the city now. On either side of the street, in both directions, shop windows glowed with a variety of the glittering atomic lighting. The street sparkled with colors, and two phalanxes of curved street lamps strode into the remote distance to the west, merging finally into a haze of light.

Marriott was pleased with the effect. It was nice living downtown, though there was a time, he recalled, when he had been ashamed of it. Judith's idea for growing a high hedge of sturdy Carrigana had cut off the house from its environment, making of it a special retreat in the very heart of the business section. Standing there at the gate, Marriott experienced a warm rebirth of regard for Judith. She had refurnished the old Marriott place, rebuilt part of it, and landscaped the grounds. It was strange to think that he had once considered her not good enough to be the wife of a Marriott. He smiled and shook his head ever so slightly. People sometimes had queer ideas about their own importance.

He closed the gate softly and walked deeper into the downtown area. A great peace lay on his spirit, a sense of the goodness of life, the rightness of things as they were. His marriage to Judith had stilled the tumult of doubt about her in his mind long ago now, and the absolute success of the marriage gave him tonight a very special sense of physical and mental completion.

Still thinking about it, he paused at the atomic-energy plant and peered through its towering plexiglass windows. The atomic powerhouse was in a cavern below the level of the street, and he looked down on it. It was a cubic monster in its special concrete and lead cellar; except for its size, it lacked glamor. By far the most interesting adjuncts of the powerhouse were the turbines that radiated from the central cube of the machine in four separate lines of three turbines, each followed by a smaller series of dynamos. In that world of titanic engines human beings looked like small toy people.

Marriott walked on. When he came to Clayton's Men's Wear, now a two-story affair of curving glass and subtle lighting, he stopped short.

That's odd, he thought. *For a moment I had the distinct impression that I used to work there.*

The night and the walk were like that. Memories of things half forgotten and fantasies that briefly seemed like memories until in amazement he rejected them as having no relation whatsoever to his life. He had married Judith in 1969, after his return from Vietnam, and they had lived an ideal married existence. In 1974 her father died, and immediately Judith's ideas about the bookstore had been put into effect. It was now a large store that employed six clerks and grossed about ninety thousand dollars a year. Before Judith the store had been lucky to make twenty thousand dollars. Judith was a wonderful businesswoman, a wonderful wife, a wonderful woman.

He was in the yard now. He paused to close the gate behind him with trembling fingers and ran up the steps of the house to the door. Still shaking, he inserted the key in the lock. He had a sense of urgency, the absolute conviction that he had to get inside as swiftly as possible. As the door shut gently behind him, he saw by the clock in the hallway that it was after midnight. He had been out longer than he intended.

The living-room lights were still on, but Judith had gone to bed. Marriott glanced around the room, baffled by its familiarity. What he had expected to find as a result of his dash had never been clear, and it was even less clear now that he had arrived at his destination. Reluctantly, he switched off the lights and went upstairs. As he passed Judith's room, which was at the head of the main staircase, she called out to him.

"You may come in and kiss me good night, dear. I'm still awake."

Marriott hesitated. "What's the matter with me?" he wondered in agony. "What am I supposed to do?"

That struck him. It was a new idea that he had a purpose on this night. That there was something . . . something at the back of his mind, he could feel. But he couldn't decide what it was.

He opened the door with the cautiousness of a man entering a woman's bedroom for the first time. Judith had a habit of sleeping without a nightdress, and he didn't want to surprise her.

A glance at the bed drained his anxiety before it came more than flashingly into his conscious mind. Judith was wearing a blue negligee. Marriott sighed his relief, but her first words made him uneasy.

"Lie down here beside me for a minute," she said.

Marriott took off his shoes, an automatic action, and stretched out on the unoccupied side of the bed. There were fragments of thoughts in his mind: One of them was a question: *What am I here for—in this future world?* It was as sharp as that, but it was gone instantly into a hidden

27

corridor of his memory. It remained wispily in the form of unhappiness. From the corners of his eyes, he studied Judith

Her face showed her age, but she had retained in her body and in her figure a measure of her youth. Her skin was clear and tanned, what he could see of it; and it was a girl's body that was silhouetted by the covering sheets. Absently, Marriott looked for the knife scar over her heart, but the nightgown, though revealing, was of opaque material and hid the area of her heart.

Marriott was disappointed. He had wanted to see the scar, definitely and determinedly wanted to see it . . . With trembling fingers, he reached over, slipped the strap from her left shoulder, and pulled the nightgown away from the scar region.

There was no scar.

His brain throbbed with surmise. Intently, he bent over her, and she must have expected a kiss, for she raised herself expectantly. He drew back, climbed off the bed, and backed toward the door.

"I'm awfully tired," he said, "I think I'll go to bed."

As he hurried out of her bedroom, he did not notice the rug just inside the doorway. He fell with a crash.

Paul Marriott, aged thirty-one, stirred and opened his eyes. He was lying face downward across the threshold of the bedroom at the head of the stairs. There was a bitter chill in the air, and it had penetrated his robe and pajamas. His body felt numb with cold.

As he sat up, he saw that it was broad daylight. *Have I been here all night?*

It was as he climbed to his feet and glanced into the bleak and unfurnished bedroom that he remembered his dream. He walked slowly down the stairs, frowning over the details. *Why did I want to see if there was a scar over her heart?* He was downstairs now, and he noticed, thrilled, that the living-room door was open.

He savored the utter emptiness of the room with relief until the icy cold air drove him to the kitchen where he hastily rekindled the fire in the stove and warmed himself at last. A glance out of the window brought another surprise. It had snowed during the night.

At Aunt Mary's Breakfast Nook he considered the problem—of himself. In his dream about the two older people he had been aware of a purpose. The purpose must have been accomplished because the couple and their world of furniture was gone.

After eating, he walked through the slushy streets trying to remember what he had learned in his solitary psychology course at college that would be helpful now. It was a dim recollection. A few words floated up: neurosis, schizoid, dementia praecox— Hard to imagine anything like that applying to himself. He had been a fool, but not—he smiled deprecatingly—insane. As an example of the former was his surprise when he discovered that factories were being built on the land adjoining his house. He had believed he was leasing it for gardening for the low sum offered. It had turned out to be the sale price. Stupid? Not really. Inexperience.

Marriott came to where he had seen the power plant in the dream. The memory was so vivid that he stopped and stared at the dozen or so dowdy frame houses that now occupied the area—each house with its half acre of land. It was easy to imagine these semi-shacks being torn down and the dazzling, transparent atomic complex rising up where they had been. He visualized the scene as he had observed it: the turbines and dynamos, coming out like begemmed spokes of a wheel from the gigantic cube of lead and concrete that was the visible portion of the "pile." The consequent structure did seem a little out of place; his vague impression was that all atomic stuff was kept far from villages small or large. In the dream, locational problems had either been solved or ignored.

A glance at his watch drew him out of his reverie. Three minutes to nine. He'd better hurry if he was going to get the store swept out before young Pete arrived.

He was a dozen feet farther along the street when he thought: *If he was going to—what?* Like a sick man he slowed his pace and dragged on, stunned. The awful memory unfolded before his mind of Paul Marriott sweeping out the Clayton store for four years. *But why? Why? What happened?*

Marriott faltered to a stop and stood leaning against a light post. The memory, such as it was, that was in his mind was pitiless. In late 1969 Paul Marriott, the last human thread of the once-thriving and important Marriott family, had suddenly lost his forward impetus, had staggered spiritually and fallen into an abyss the nature and depth of which was still blurred in mist. In a frenzy of self-abnegation he had allowed himself to be swindled out of the valuable Marriott land and had humiliated his name and person by becoming the sweeper and the clerk at Clayton's Men's Wear.

But what happened to Judith? Marriott shook his head with a numb sense of imminent revelation. He recalled that Judith and he had been engaged. Then—

His brain was registering unevenly as if the thought on the edge of his consciousness was too big for it. He remembered the question Judith's father had asked the day before. ". . . What started you thinking about her, Paul?"

That hypnotist! Marriott made the positive identification. The man had put him under as a part of his show and had stirred up his subconscious. . . . *I've got to see him . . .*

The search was like a dream, his mind darting always faster than his feet and snatching him rudely from half-finished conversations. He had memories of expressmen, bus drivers, theater managers, and hotel clerks gazing after him with offended eyes and frowning faces. He was a man who could not pause for the amenities, but the memory of his madness was mercifully vague, and so it mattered not. At two in the afternoon, when the dulling sky was brighter than it had been in the earlier part of the day, he walked into one more hotel, asked the question—and had his man.

Offstage, Blandar the Magnificent was not quite as Marriott remembered him. He looked smaller and, in his conventional blue suit, unimposing. Under other circumstances Marriott might have guessed him to be a salesman.

"You would like to buy me a drink?" he said.

The intention had not occurred to Marriott, but he made it his own. As they walked into the bar, he found himself explaining the difficult time he had had. "I've easily traveled a hundred miles since I left Hampden."

He saw that Blandar was not going to apologize for his elusiveness. He waited impatiently as the drinks were set up. Blandar drained his with a gulp. "Another," he said to the bartender. He sipped that one more slowly, but Marriott, who was beginning to guess Blandar's own difficulty, discreetly left the change from his ten-dollar bill on the counter.

"I seem to remember you now," Blandar said when Marriott had explained his problem. "You were reluctant to come up, but the young men were determined. I caught an undertone of—" He cocked his head and hesitated—"of unconscious desire to humiliate you."

He added, "I used to be a practicing psychologist until I discovered I could make more money as a traveling hypnotist—so I didn't play up to their neuroticism."

Marriott nodded. He had come to the conclusion that the desire to humiliate him was unconscious. "Everybody," he said, "has been outwardly kind to me. I suppose people always like to see someone they've envied taken down a peg. But what I don't understand is why did I acquiesce in the degradation?"

"*Guilt.*"

Marriott could feel himself changing color. "What do you mean?"

He seemed to be in a well of darkness staring up into the light at the other man. The hypnotist's eyes were unwinking. "This girl, Judith," he said, "when did you last see her?"

"Why—I don't remember." He was swaying. *Funny, I feel as if I'm going to faint.*

"The nature of your hallucination," Blandar said, "opens up one more potentiality of hypnotism. Personally, I have yet to find the end of its many possibilities. Most people escape into amnesia or into the past when they meet a situation they cannot face. Your first move *was* amnesia, but when you started to come out of that, you were confronted by a problem. In your case the past was a very special one. Those were the days when your family was important. Couldn't solve your guilt there. So you looked for your answer in the future." Blandar frowned. "Tell me that part again. It sounded . . . unlifelike . . . to me. But I can't quite put my finger on it."

It was like drawing aside a curtain to a secret room, as if his mind had an awful suspicion that it was going to be penetrated to the uttermost. Blandar sipped two drinks while he listened and another drink while he thought it over.

"I have a habit," he said at last, "of telling a deep trance subject that the next time he gives me permission to hypnotize him he'll go under when I snap my fingers and say, 'Sleep!' I don't recall doing that to you, but I must have. May I hypnotize you?"

"What are you going to do?" There was dread in Marriott's voice.

"Find out what happened."

"You can do it through hypnotism?"

"Every detail will come out."

Marriott fought an impulse to run. "Here?" he said faintly. They were sitting on stools at the bar.

Blandar said, "Let's go over to the end booth." A moment later, Marriott said heavily, "Yes, you may hypnotize me." Blandar said, "Sleep!" And snapped his fingers.

Marriott's eyes shut tight, and he waited. At last, puzzled, he opened his eyes. "Didn't seem to work," he began. He stopped, stunned. There was no sign of Blandar. A note lay on the table in front of him. He picked it up and read:

Dear Marriott:

It was your high regard for Judith in the "future" hallucination that made me think something was wrong. It fitted in with your admission (also in the illusion) that you had once considered her unworthy for a Marriott. For some reason you were anxious to make up to her for that opinion, too anxious considering that your thought must at all times have been secret. But it was the unqualified admiration you had for her that made me suspect the truth. Interesting, too, was that the only way you dared look for the scar was to shove it twenty years ahead in time, and even then you wouldn't admit its existence.

I don't pretend to explain your vision of an atomic world. It sounds very real to me, and I suggest you remember as many details as you can.

But now for the finale. You will have a return of memory when you open your gate this evening. The moment you have seen what I have willed you to see, go to . . . and here I pause. My reason says, go to the office of the sheriff. (I gather he was a friend of your father's.) Unfortunately, there's another factor. The other man. He was never found, or seen. But when I had you under hypnosis, suddenly he spoke to me out of your unconscious. Your voice changed, grew sing-song; and this stranger said, "Blandar, let it happen free-ly. At the moment of awareness, I promise to reveal myself to Paul Marriott . . . and free us both—"

What does one say to a suggestion like that from the hypnotized subject? I made several efforts to obtain an explanation. But I got nothing more.

Well, Mr. Marriott, I've done my best for you. To protect myself, I've ordered you to destroy this note ten minutes after you first read it.

Good luck.

B.

Marriott stopped before the gate. It was almost dark, and the shadows of foliage lay long and black over the wet street. The house loomed up incongruously in the twilight. In its day it had been beautiful, and (Marriott told himself) he would see to it that it was again, but first it would have to go through a purgatory of being a rooming house. He had to have money. There was property that he wanted to buy where the atomic plant would be built in the not too distant future. And he must try to recall just what businesses had been prospering in his vision of the future.

It seemed to him, too, that a good lawyer might help him gain fair value for the land he had sold in the belief that he was only leasing. A sick man must surely have legal rights.

The plans seethed in his mind in spite of what Blandar had said. *What can possibly happen when I open the gate?* To that extent his mind had rationalized.

Yet, fingers on gate, he hesitated. The twilight deepened measurably. He braced himself—and pushed. The gate creaked open. Marriott stepped across it expectantly. *Whatever it is,* he told himself, *will only be in my mind.*

He walked a dozen feet toward the veranda steps, then paused in disappointment. Isn't the *posthypnotic* suggestion he gave me going to?—

He had half turned; and one foot was slightly raised off the ground. In that position he froze. A woman's naked body was lying under the brush near the gate. Judith.

In the semidarkness, she was strangely silhouetted, every part of her body shown clearly. Her face was aglow as from an inner light. The gleam of something metallic protruding from her heart was plainly visible.

The man who had been lying beside her stood up with a sudden, agile motion, as if he were lighter than his body size indicated. Much lighter, or *much* stronger. He leaped toward Marriott, seeming to bound forward with catlike legs.

He teetered to a graceful stop on his toes. Marriott had a glimpse, then, of eyes of bright, shining blue and of a face that was long and narrow like the body. The whole effect was of someone intensely alive.

The light from the nearby street lamp glowed upon the stranger. And it was that that made it possible for Marriott to know that what happened next was . . . fantastic.

Words came from the man—but his mouth did not open; his lips did not move. "By killing herself she created an energy field that affected me, also. And so we were all three of us—you and she and I—caught in a time stasis."

Marriott said nothing; he couldn't. The entire dialogue seemed without meaning. Worse, he had the abrupt awareness that he had heard no sound. The night was still. Only a few faint echoes came to him, and those all from a distance: a faraway motor car; the chirping of a night bird; the stirring of a breeze in the trees at the far end of the yard.

"Usually," said the man's thoughts into his mind, "because of my total ability at mental control, a woman accepts me instantly. That's particularly true of these early human types who are not conscious of the neural processes involved. This one started to accept me, but at the critical moment she had a deep adverse reaction. At once it became in her a mind a rape situation. She grabbed my time needle and stabbed herself with it. Naturally she thought of you as she died, and so I was doubly trapped. I made an attempt to save her by projecting her forward in time, literally recreated her body in a parallel time world—"

The thought that was in Marriott's mind was that *he* knew why she had killed herself. *His* attitude. She had detected in him the feeling of a Marriott being better. She had accordingly set a special standard for herself; and at

the moment of being violated, realizing she was being reduced in value below the Marriott level, in a spasm of despair she struck the mortal blow.

The insight was completed and was gone. He realized next
that he was not up to all of the communication that had
been thrown at him. But he did comprehend one meaning:
This is the man responsible for Judith's death!

As he had that realization, he jumped and grabbed.

Caught a whirlwind!

His fingers clutched at a naked body that actually felt
hard, as if the muscles under the skin were metal. As he
tried to hold, hands that were stone-hard struck at his
wrists with bone-breaking impact. Marriott uttered a bray
of pain, but his purpose, his awful impulse to hurt and
damage and maim, remained like a knot inside him.

Total violence! He lunged forward and struck with all
his strength at the face; felt his bare fist crash into it. The
stranger screamed and retreated, bounding, bouncing back.

"You fool!" The thought slammed into Marriott's brain.
"I was trying to hold myself here long enough to free you
from that alternate world. Now it's too late."

The man had retreated into the shadow beside the house.
He stopped. He was dimly visible, but there was a shim-
mering effect that was hard on Marriott's eyes. He closed
them hard. When he opened them, the other man was gone.

Marriott staggered toward the emptiness, refusing to believe there was nothing there. And so he clutched at darkness as if it had substance, lost his balance, and ended up
sprawled on one knee and with his hands hard-thrust against
the grass.

Slowly, reluctantly accepting the departure . . . and
beginning to have a dim consciousness of the many meanings that had been thrust at him, he climbed to his feet and
walked unsteadily to the front door.

As he opened it and stepped inside, the voice of Judith
came to him from the living room. "Is that you, dear?"

Marriott could feel himself relaxing . . . *Of course,* he
thought, *this is where I am*—and where he would be from
now on, thank God.

"Yes, my darling," he called. "It's me."

He walked forward into the house, closing the door behind him.

THE RAT
AND THE SNAKE

MARK GRAY's main pleasure in life was feeding rats to his pet python. He kept the python in a blocked-off room in the old house in which he lived alone. Each mealtime, he would put the rat in a narrow tunnel he had rigged. At the end of the tunnel was an opening. The rat, going through the narrow space into the bright room beyond, automatically spring-locked a gate across the opening.

It would then find itself in the room with the python, with no way of escape.

Mark liked to listen to its squeaks as it became aware of its danger, and then he would hear its mad scurrying to escape the irresistible enemy. Sometimes he watched the exciting scene through a plate-glass window, but he actually preferred the sound to the fight, conjuring his own delectable mental pictures, always from the viewpoint of the python.

During World War III, the O.P.A. forgot to put a ceiling price on rats. The catching of rats got no special priority. Rat catchers were drafted into the armed forces as readily as the other people. The supply of rats grew less. Mark was soon reduced to catching his own rats; but he had to work for a living in the ever-leaner times of war, so that there were periods of time when the python was fed infrequently.

Then one day Mark, ever searching, glimpsed some white rats through a window of an old commercial-style building.

He peered in eagerly, and though the room was dimly lighted with wartime regulation bulbs, he was able to make out that it was a large room with hundreds of cages in it and that each of the cages contained rats.

He made it to the front of the building at a dead run. In pausing to catch his breath, he noticed the words on the door: CARRON LABORATORIES, Research.

He found himself presently in a dim hallway of a business office. Because everybody was clearly working twice as hard because of the war, it took a little while to attract the attention of one of the women employees; and there were other delays such as just sitting and waiting while it seemed as if he was the forgotten man. But after all those minutes he was finally led into the office of a small, tight-faced man, who was introduced as Eric Plode and who listened to his request and the reason for it.

When Mark described his poor, starving python, the small man laughed a sudden, explosive laughter. But his eyes remained cold. Moments later he curtly rejected the request.

Whereupon he made a personal thing out of it. "And don't get any ideas," he snarled. "Stay away from our rats. If we catch you filching around here, we'll have the law on you."

Until those words were spoken, Mark hadn't really thought about becoming a rat-stealing criminal. Except for his peculiar love for his python, he was a law-abiding, tax-paying nobody.

As Mark was leaving, Plode hastily sent a man to follow him. Then, smiling grimly, he walked into an office that had printed on the door: HENRY CARRON, Private.

"Well, Hank," he said gaily, "I think we've got our subject."

Carron said, "This had better be good since we can't even get prisoners of war assigned us for the job."

The remark made Plode frown a little. He had a tendency toward ironic thoughts, and he had often thought recently, "Good God, they're going to use the process on millions of the unsuspecting enemy after we get it tested, but they won't give us a G.D. so-and-so to try it out on because of some kind of prisoner of war convention."

Aloud, he said smugly, "I suppose by a stretch of the imagination you could call him human."

"*That bad?*"

Plode described Mark and his hobby, finished, "I suppose it's a matter of point of view. But I won't feel any guilt, particularly if he sneaks over tonight and with criminal intent tries to steal some of our rats." He grinned mirthlessly. "Can you think of anything lower than a rat stealer?"

Henry Carron hesitated but only for moments. Millions of people were dead and dying, and a test absolutely had to be made on a human being. Because if something went wrong on the battlefield, the effect of surprise might be lost with who knew what repercussions.

"One thing sure," he nodded, "there'll be no evidence against us. So go ahead."

It seemed to Mark, as he came stealthily back that night, that these people with their thousands of rats would never miss the equivalent of one rat a week or so. He was especially pleased when he discovered that the window was unlocked and that the menagerie was unguarded. No doubt, he thought good-humoredly, babysitters for rats were in scarce supply because of the wartime worker shortage.

The next day he thrilled again to the familiar sound of a rat squeaking in fear of the python. Toward evening his phone rang. It was Eric Plode.

"I warned you," said the small man in a vicious tone. "Now you must pay the penalty."

Plode felt better for having issued the warning. "Be it on his own soul," he said sanctimoniously, "if he's there."

Mark hung up, contemptuous. Let them try to prove anything.

In his sleep that night he seemed to be suffocating. He woke up, and he was not lying on his bed but instead was on a hard floor. He groped for the light switch but could not find it. There was a bright rectangle of light about twenty feet away. He headed for it.

Crash! A gate slammed shut behind him as he emerged.

He was in a vast room, larger than anything he had ever seen. Yet it was vaguely familiar. Except for its size it resembled the room in which he kept his python.

On the floor in front of him, an object that he had noticed and regarded as some sort of a leathery rug, thicker than he was tall, stirred and moved toward him.

Realization came suddenly, horrendously.

He was the size of a rat. This was the python slithering across the floor with distended jaws.

Mad squealing as Mark Gray experienced the ultimate thrill of the strange method by which he had enjoyed life for so many years . . . Experienced it this one and only time from the viewpoint of the rat.

THE BARBARIAN

IN HIS INITIAL ADDRESS to the Patronate, following his return from Venus, Tews said among other things, "It is difficult for us to realize, but Linn is now without formidable enemies anywhere. Our opponents on Mars and Venus having been decisively defeated by our forces in the past two decades, we are now in a unique historical position: the sole great power in the world of man. A period of unlimited peace and creative reconstruction seems inevitable."

He returned to the palace with the cheers of the Patronate ringing in his ears, his mood one of thoughtful jubilation. His spies had already reported that the patrons gave him a great deal of the credit for the victory on Venus. After all, the war had dragged on for a long time before his arrival. And then, abruptly, almost overnight, it had ended. The conclusion was that his brilliant leadership had made a decisive contribution. It required no astuteness for Tews to realize that, under such circumstances, he could generously bestow a triumph on Jerrin, and lose nothing by the other's honors.

Despite his own words to the Patronate, he found himself, as the peaceful weeks went by, progressively amazed at the reality of what he had said: no enemies. Nothing to fear. Even yet, it seemed hard to believe that the universe belonged to Linn; and that, as the Lord Adviser, he was now in his own sphere in a position of power over more subjects than any man had ever been. So it seemed to the dazzled Tews.

He would be a devoted leader, of course—he reassured himself hastily, disowning the momentary pride. He visualized great works that would reflect the glory of Linn and the golden age of Tews. The vision was so noble and inspiring that for long he merely toyed with hazy, magnificent plans and took no concrete action of any kind.

He was informed presently that Clane had returned from Venus. Shortly thereafter he received a message from the mutation.

His Excellency,
Lord Adviser Tews
My most honored uncle:

I should like to visit you and describe to you the result of several conversations between my brother Jerrin and myself concerning potential dangers for the empire. They do not seem severe, but we are both concerned about the preponderance of slaves as against citizens on Earth, and we are unhappy about our lack of knowledge of the present situation among the peoples of the moons of Jupiter and Saturn.

Since these are the only dangers in sight, the sooner we examine every aspect of the problem the more certain we can be that the destiny of Linn will be under the control of intelligent action and not governed in future by the necessary opportunism that has been for so many generations the main element of government.

Your obedient nephew,
Clane

The letter irritated Tews. It seemed meddlesome. It reminded him that his control of Linn and of the glorious future he envisaged for the empire was not complete, that in fact these nephews might urge compromises that would dim the beauty that only he, apparently, could see. Nevertheless, his reply was diplomatic:

My dear Clane:

It was a pleasure to hear from you, and as soon as I return from the mountains, I shall be happy to receive you and discuss all these matters in the most thoroughgoing fashion. I have instructed various departments to gather data so that when we do get together, we can talk on the basis of facts.

Tews,
Lord Adviser

He actually issued the instructions and actually listened to a brief account from an official who was an "expert" concerning conditions on the moons of Jupiter and Saturn. They were all inhabited by tribes in various stages of barbaric culture. Recent reports gleaned from questioning of primitives who came from there and from the Linnan traders who visited certain ports of entry indicated that the old game of intrigue and murder among tribal chieftains seeking ascendancy was still going on.

Relieved in spite of his previous conviction that the situation was exactly as it was now described, Tews departed on his mountain vacation with a retinue of three hundred courtiers and five hundred slaves. He was still there a month later when a second message arrived from Clane.

Most gracious Lord Adviser Tews:

Your response to my message was a great relief to me. I wonder if I could further impose upon your good offices and have your department heads determine how many are still here and where they are presently concentrated. The reason for this inquiry is that I have discovered that several of my agents on Europa, the great moon of Jupiter, were suddenly executed about a year ago and that actually my own information from that territory is based upon reports, all of which are not less than two years old, and those are extremely vague. It seems that about five years ago a new leader began to unify Europa; and my agents' reports—when I now examine the data they furnished—grew less clear with each month after that. I suspect that I have been victimized by carefully prepared propaganda. If this be so, the fact that somebody was astute enough to seize my channels of information worries me.

These are only suspicions, of course, but it would

seem advisable to have your people make inquiries with the possibility in mind that our present information sources are unreliable.

Your faithful servant, and nephew,
Clane

The reference to the mutation's "agents" reminded Tews unpleasantly that he lived in a world of spies. *I suppose,* he thought wearily, *propaganda is even now being circulated against me because I am on a vacation. People cannot possibly realize what great plans my engineers and I are making for the State on this so-called pleasure trip.*

He wondered if, by releasing a series of public statements about the grandiose future, he might successfully head off criticism.

That irritation lasted for a day, and then he read Clane's letter again and decided that an unruffled and diplomatic approach was desirable. He must ever be in a position to say that he invariably took the most thorough precaution against any eventuality.

He gave the necessary instructions, advised Clane that he had done so—and then began to consider seriously the situation that would exist when Jerrin returned from Venus six or eight months hence to receive his triumph. It no longer seemed quite the satisfactory prospect that it had been when he himself had first returned from Venus. These nephews of his tended to interfere in State affairs, and indeed both had the legal right to be advisers of the government. Each, according to law, had a Council vote in Linnan affairs, although neither could directly interfere with administration.

I suppose, Tews grudgingly acknowledged to himself, *Clane is within his rights; but what was it mother once said: "It is an unwise man who always exercises his rights."* He laughed, grimacing.

That night, just before he went to sleep, Tews had a flash of insight: *I'm slipping back into suspicion—the same fears that disturbed me when I was on Venus. I'm being influenced by this damnable palace atmosphere.*

He felt personally incapable of base thoughts, and accepted their presence in others—he told himself—with the greatest reluctance, and then only because of the possible effect on the State.

His sense of duty—that was the real pressure on him, he felt convinced. It compelled him to be aware of, and actually to look for, scheming and plotting, even though he was revolted by any indications of intrigue.

The realization of his own fundamental integrity reassured Tews. *After all,* he thought, *I may occasionally be misled, but I cannot be wrong if I remain constantly on the alert for danger from all sources. And even a mutation with scientific knowledge and weapons is a matter about which I, as guardian of the State, must take cognizance.*

He had already given considerable thought to the weapons he had seen Clane use on Venus. And during the days that followed he came to the conclusion that he must take action. He kept saying to himself how reluctant he was to do so, but finally he advised Clane:

My dear nephew:

Although you have evidently not felt free to ask for the protection to which your rank and the value of your work entitles you, I am sure you will be happy to hear that the State is prepared to undertake protection of the material that you have rescued from the pits of the gods and from other ancient sources.

The safest place for all this material is at your residence in Linn. Accordingly, I am authorizing funds to transport to the city any such equipment that you have at your country estate. A guards unit will arrive at the estate within the week with adequate transport, and another guards unit is this day taking up guard duty at your town residence.

The captain of the guard, while of course responsible to me, will naturally grant you every facility for carrying on your work.

It is with pleasure, my dear Clane, that I extend to you this costly but earned protection.

At some time not too far in the future I should like to have the privilege of a personally conducted tour so that I may see for myself what treasures you have in

your collection, with a view to finding further uses for
them for the general welfare.

> With cordial best wishes
> Tews,
> Lord Adviser

At least, thought Tews, after he had dispatched the message and given the necessary orders to the military forces,
*that will for the present get the material all in one place.
Later, a further more stringent control is always possible—
not that it will ever be necessary, of course.*

The wise leader simply planned for any contingency. Even
the actions of his most dearly beloved relatives must be examined objectively.

He learned presently that Clane had offered no resistance
and that the material had been transported to Linn without
incident.

He was still at the mountain palace of the Linns when a
third letter arrived from Clane. Though briefly stated, it
was a major social document. The preamble read:

To our uncle, the Lord Adviser:
   It being the considered opinion of Lords Jerrin and
Clane Linn that a dangerous preponderance of slaves
exists in Linn and that indeed the condition of slavery
is wholly undesirable in a healthy State, it is herewith
proposed that Lord Adviser Tews during his government lay down as a guiding rule for future generations
the following principles:
   1. All law-abiding human beings are entitled to the
free control of their own persons.
   2. Where free control does not now obtain, it shall
be delivered to the individual on a rising scale, the
first two steps of which shall become effective immediately.
   3. The first step shall be that no slave shall in future
be physically punished except by the order of a court.
   4. The second step shall be that the slave's work day
shall not in future exceed ten hours.

The other steps outlined a method of gradually freeing
the slaves until after twenty years only incorrigibles would

be "not free," and all of these would be controlled by the State itself under laws whereby each was dealt with "as an individual."

Tews read the document with amazement and amusement. He recalled another saying of his mother's: "Don't ever worry about the idealists. The mob will cut their throats at the proper moment."

His amusement faded rapidly. *These boys are really interfering in the affairs of state in Linn itself, which is only remotely in their province.* As, the summer over, he made preparations to return to the city, Tews scowlingly considered the threat "to the State," which—it seemed to him —was building up with alarming speed.

On the second day after his return to Linn he received another letter from Clane. This one requested an audience to discuss "those matters relating to the defense of the empire, about which your departments have been gathering information."

What infuriated Tews about the letter was that the mutation was not even giving him time to settle down after his return. True, the work of reestablishment did not involve him—but it was a matter of courtesy to the office he held. On that level, Tews decided in an icy rage, Clane's persistence bore all the earmarks of a deliberate insult.

He sent a curt note in reply, which stated simply:

My dear Clane:
   I will advise you as soon as I am free of the more pressing problems of administration. Please await word from me.

Tews

He slept that night, confident that he was at last taking a firm stand and that it was about time.

He awoke to news of disaster.

The only warning was a steely glinting of metal in the early-morning sky. The invaders swooped down on the city of Linn in three hundred spaceships. There must have been advance spying, for they landed in force at the gates that were heavily guarded and at the main troop barracks inside the city. From each ship debouched two hundred-odd men.

"Sixty thousand soldiers!" said Lord Adviser Tews after

47

he had studied the reports. He issued instructions for the defense of the palace and sent a carrier pigeon to the three legions encamped outside the city, ordering two of them to attack when ready. And then he sat pale but composed, watching the spectacle from a window that overlooked the hazy vastness of Linn proper.

Everything was vague and unreal. Most of the invading ships had disappeared behind large buildings. A few lay in the open, but they looked dead. It was hard to grasp that vicious fighting was going on in their vicinity. At nine o'clock, a messenger arrived from the Lady Lydia:

> Dear Son:
>   Have you any news? Who is attacking us? Is it a limited assault or an invasion of the empire? Have you contacted Clane?
>
> L.

The first prisoner was brought in while Tews was scowling over the unpalatable suggestion that he seek the advice of his relative. The mutation was the last person he wanted to see. The prisoner, a bearded giant, proudly confessed that he was from Europa, one of the moons of Jupiter, and that he feared neither man nor god. The man's size and obvious physical prowess startled Tews. But his naïve outlook on life was cheering. Subsequent prisoners had similar physical and mental characteristics. And so, long before noon, Tews had a fairly clear picture of the situation.

This was a barbarian invasion from Europa. It was obviously for loot only. But unless he acted swiftly, Linn would be divested in a few days of treasures garnered over the centuries. Bloodthirsty commands flowed from Tews' lips. Put all prisoners to the sword. Destroy their ships, their weapons, their clothing. Leave not one vestige of their presence to pollute the eternal city.

The morning ran its slow course. Tews considered making an inspection of the city escorted by the palace cavalry. He abandoned the plan when he realized it would be impossible for commanders to send him reports if he were on the move. For the same reason he could not transfer his headquarters to a less clearly marked building. Just before noon, the relieving report arrived that two of three camp legions were attacking in force at the main gates.

The news steadied him. He began to think in terms of broader, more basic information about what had happened. He remembered unhappily that his departments probably had the information that—spurred by Clane—he had asked for months ago. Hastily, he called in several experts and sat somberly while each of the men in turn told what he had learned.

There was actually a great deal of data. Europa, the great moon of Jupiter, had been inhabited from legendary times by fiercely quarreling tribes. Its vast atmosphere was said to have been created artificially with the help of the atom gods by the scientists of the golden age. Like all the artificial atmosphere, it contained a high proportion of the gas, teneol, which admitted sunlight but did not allow much heat to escape into space.

Starting about five years before, travelers had begun to bring out reports of a leader named Czinczar who was ruthlessly welding all the hating factions of the planet into one nation. For a while it was such a dangerous territory that traders landed only at specified ports of entry. The information they received was that Czinczar's attempt at unification had failed. Contact grew even more vague after that; and it was clear to the listening Tews that the new leader had actually succeeded in his conquests and that any word to the contrary was propaganda. The cunning Czinczar had seized outgoing communication sources and confused them while he consolidated his position among the barbarous forces of the planet.

Czinczar. The name had a sinister rhythm to it, a ring of leashed violence, a harsh, metallic tintinnabulation. If such a man and his followers escaped with even a fraction of the portable wealth of Linn, the inhabited solar system would echo with the exploit. The government of Lord Adviser Tews might tumble like a house of cards.

Tews had been hesitating. There was a plan in his mind that would work better if carried out in the dead of night. But that meant giving the attackers precious extra hours for loot. He decided not to wait, but dispatched a command to the third—still unengaged—camp legion to enter the tunnel that led into the central palace.

49

As a precaution, and with the hope of distracting the enemy leader, he sent a message to Czinczar in the care of a captured barbarian officer. In it he pointed out the foolishness of an attack that could only result in bloody reprisals on Europa itself and suggested that there was still time for an honorable withdrawal. There was only one thing wrong with all these schemings. Czinczar had concentrated a large force of his own for the purpose of capturing the Imperial party. And had held back in the hope that he would learn definitely whether or not the Lord Adviser was inside the palace. The released prisoner, who delivered Tews' message, established his presence inside.

The attack in force that followed captured the Central Palace and everyone in it, and surprised the legionnaires who were beginning to emerge from the secret passageway. Czinczar's men poured all the oil in the large palace tanks into the downward sloping passageway and set it afire.

Thus died an entire legion of men.

That night a hundred reserve barbarian spaceships landed behind the Linnan soldiers besieging the gates. And in the morning, when the barbarians inside the city launched an attack, the two remaining legions were cut to pieces.

Of these events the Lord Adviser Tews knew nothing. His skull had been turned over the previous day to Czinczar's favorite goldsmith, to be plated with Linnan gold and shaped into a goblet to celebrate the greatest victory of the century.

To Lord Clane Linn, going over his accounts on his country estate, the news of the fall of Linn came as a special shock. With unimportant exceptions, all his atomic material was in Linn. He dismissed the messenger, who had unwisely shouted the news as he entered the door of the accounting department. And then sat at his desk—and realized that he had better accept for the time being the figures of his slave bookkeepers on the condition of the estate.

As he glanced around the room after announcing the postponement, it seemed to him that at least one of the slaves showed visible relief. He did not delay, but called the man before him instantly. He had an inexorable system in dealing with slaves, a system inherited from his long-dead mentor, Joquin, along with the estate itself.

Integrity, hard work, loyalty, and a positive attitude produced better conditions, shorter working hours, more freedom of action, after thirty the right to marry, after forty legal freedom. Laziness and other negative attitudes such as cheating were punished by a set pattern of demotions. Short of changing the law of the land, Clane could not at the moment imagine a better system in view of the existence of slavery. And now, in spite of his personal anxieties, he carried out the precept of Joquin as it applied to a situation where no immediate evidence was available. He told the man, Oorag, what had aroused his suspicions and asked him if they were justified. "If you are guilty and confess," he said, "you will receive only one demotion. If you do not confess and you are later proven guilty, there will be three demotions, which means physical labor, as you know."

The slave, a big man, shrugged and said with a sneer, "By the time Czinczar is finished with you Linnans, you will be working for me."

"Field labor," said Clane curtly, "for three months, ten hours a day."

It was no time for mercy. An empire under attack did not flinch from the harshest acts. Anything that could be construed as weakness would be disastrous.

As the slave was led out by guards, he shouted a final insult over his shoulder. "You wretched mutation," he said, "you'll be where you belong when Czinczar gets here."

Clane did not answer. He considered it doubtful that the new conqueror had been selected by fate to punish all the evildoers of Linn according to their desserts. It would take too long. He put the thought out of his mind and walked to the doorway. There he paused and faced the dozen trusted slaves who sat at their various desks.

"Do nothing rash," he said slowly in a clear voice, "any of you. If you harbor emotions similar to those expressed by Oorag, restrain yourselves. The fall of one city in a surprise attack is not important." He hesitated. He was, he realized, appealing to their cautious instincts, but his reason told him that in a great crisis men did not always consider all the potentialities.

"I am aware," he said finally, "there is no great pleasure

in being a slave, though it has advantages—economic security, free craft training. But Oorag's wild words are a proof that if young slaves were free to do as they pleased, they would constitute a jarring, if not revolutionary factor in the community. It is unfortunately true that people of different races can only gradually learn to live together."

He went out, satisfied that he had done the best possible under the circumstances. He had no doubt whatsoever that here, in this defiance of Oorag, the whole problem of a slave empire had again shown itself in miniature. If Czinczar were to conquer any important portion of Earth, a slave uprising would follow automatically. There were too many slaves, far too many for safety, in the Linnan empire.

Outside, he saw his first refugees. They were coming down near the main granaries in a variety of colorful sky-scooters. Clane watched them for a moment, trying to picture their departure from Linn. The amazing thing was that they had waited till the forenoon of the second day. People must simply have refused to believe that the city was in danger, though, of course, early fugitives could have fled in other directions. And so not come near the estate.

Clane emerged decisively out of his reverie. He called a slave and dispatched him to the scene of the arrivals with a command to his personal guards. "Tell these people who have rapid transportation to keep moving. Here, eighty miles from Linn, we shall take care only of the foot-weary."

Briskly now, he went into his official residence and called the commanding officer of his troops. "I want volunteers," he explained, "particularly men with strong religious beliefs who on this second night after the invasion are prepared to fly into Linn and remove all the transportable equipment from my laboratory."

His plan, as he outlined it finally to some forty volunteers, was simplicity itself. In the confusion of taking over a vast city it would probably be several days before the barbarian army would actually occupy all the important residences. Particularly, on these early days, they might miss a house situated, as his was, behind a barrier of trees.

If by some unfortunate chance it was already occupied, it would probably be so loosely held that bold men could easily kill every alien on the premises and so accomplish their purpose.

"I want to impress upon you," Clane went on, "the importance of this task. As all of you know, I am a member of the temple hierarchy. I have been entrusted with sacred god metals and sacred equipment, including material taken from the very homes of the gods. It would be a disaster if these precious relics were to fall into unclean hands. I, therefore, charge you that if you should by some mischance be captured, do not reveal the real purpose of your presence. Say that you came to rescue your owner's private property. Even admit you were foolish to sacrifice yourself for such a reason."

Mindful of Tews' guard unit, he finished his instructions. "It may be that Linnan soldiers are guarding the equipment, in which case give the officer in command this letter."

He handed the document to the captain of the volunteers. It was an authorization signed by Clane with the seal of his rank. Since the death of Tews, such an authorization would not be lightly ignored.

When they had gone out to prepare for the mission, Clane dispatched one of his private spaceships to the nearby city of Goram and asked the commander there, a friend of his, what kind of counteraction was being prepared against the invader. "Are the authorities in the cities and towns," he asked, "showing that they understand the patterns of action required of them in a major emergency? Or must the old law be explained to them from the beginning?"

The answer arrived in the shortest possible time, something under forty minutes. The general placed his forces at Clane's command and advised that he had dispatched messengers to every major city on Earth in the name of "his excellency, Lord Clane Linn, ranking survivor on Earth of the noble Tews, the late Lord Adviser, who perished at the head of his troops, defending the city of Linn from the foul and murderous surprise attack launched by a barbarian horde of beastlike men who seek to destroy the fairest civilization that ever existed."

There was more in the same vein, but it was not the excess of verbiage that startled Clane. It was the offer itself and the implications. *In his name* an army was being organized.

After rereading the message, he walked slowly to the

full-length mirror in the adjoining bathroom and stared at his image. He was dressed in the fairly presentable reading gown of a temple scientist. Like all his temple clothing, the shoulder cloth folds of this concealed his "differences" from casual view. An observer would have to be very acute to see how carefully the cloak was drawn around his neck, and how it was built up to hide the slant of his body from the neck down, and how tightly the arm ends were tied together at his wrists.

It would take three months to advise Lord Jerrin on Venus and four to reach Lord Draid on Mars, both planets being on the far side of the sun from Earth. It would require almost, but not quite, twice as long to receive a message from them. Only a member of the ruling family could possibly win the support of the diversified elements of the empire. Of the fate of the Lord Adviser's immediate family, there was as yet no word. Besides, they were women. Which left Lord Clane, youngest brother of Jerrin, grandson of the late Lord Leader. For not less than six months accordingly he would be the acting Lord Leader of Linn.

The afternoon of that second day of the invasion waned slowly. Great ships began to arrive, bringing soldiers. By dusk, more than a thousand men were encamped along the road to the city of Linn and by the riverside. Darting small craft and the wary full-sized spaceships floated overhead, and foot patrols were out, guarding all approaches to the estate.

The roads themselves were virtually deserted. It was too soon for the mobs from Linn, which air-scooter scouts reported were fleeing the captured city by the gates that, at midafternoon, were still open.

During the last hour before dark, the air patrols reported that the gates were being shut one by one. And that the stream of refugees was dwindling to a trickle near the darkening city. All through that last hour, the sky was free of scooters transporting refugees. It seemed clear that the people who could afford the costly machines were either already safe or had waited too long, possibly in the hope of succoring some absent member of the family.

At midnight the volunteers departed on their dangerous mission in ten scooters and one spaceship. As a first gesture of his new authority Clane augmented their forces by adding a hundred soldiers from the regular army. He watched the shadowy ships depart, then hurried to attend a meeting of those general officers who had had time to arrive. A dozen men climbed to their feet as he entered. They saluted, then stood at attention.

Clane stopped short. He had intended to be calm, matter-of-fact, pretending even to himself that what was happening was natural. The feeling wasn't like that. An emotion came, familiar, terrifying. He could feel it tingling up the remoter reflexes of his nervous system as of old, the beginning of the dangerous childish panic, product of his early, horrible days as a tormented mutation. The muscles of his face worked. Three times he swallowed with difficulty. Then, with a stiff gesture, he returned the salute. And walking hastily to the head of the table, he sat down.

Clane waited till they had seated themselves, then asked for brief reports as to available troops. He noted down the figures given by each man for his province and at the end added up the columns.

"With four provinces still to be heard from," he announced, "we have a total of eighteen thousand trained soldiers, six thousand partly trained reserves, and some five hundred thousand able-bodied civilians."

"Your excellency," said his friend Morkid, "the Linnan empire maintains normally a standing army of one million men. On Earth by far the greatest forces were stationed in or near the city of Linn, and they have been annihilated. Some four hundred thousand men are still on Venus and slightly more than two hundred thousand on Mars."

Clane, who had been mentally adding up the figures given, said quickly, "That doesn't add up to a million men."

Morkid nodded gravely. "For the first time in years, the army is under strength. The conquest of Venus seemed to eliminate all potential enemies of Linn, and Lord Adviser Tews considered it a good time to economize."

"I see," said Clane. He felt pale and bloodless, like a man who has suddenly discovered that he cannot walk by himself.

Lydia climbed heavily out of her sedan chair, conscious of how old and unattractive she must seem to the grinning barbarians in the courtyard. She didn't let it worry her too much. She had been old a long time now, and her image in a mirror no longer shocked her. The important thing was that her request for an interview had been granted by Czinczar after she had, at his insistence, withdrawn the proviso that she be given a safe conduct.

The old woman smiled mirthlessly. She no longer valued highly the combination of skin and bones that was her body. But there was exhilaration in the realization that she was probably going to her death. Despite her age and some self-disgust, she felt reluctant to accept oblivion. But Clane had asked her to take the risk. It vaguely amazed Lydia that the idea of the mutation's holding the Lord Leadership did not dismay her any more. She had her own private reasons for believing Clane capable. She walked slowly along the familiar hallways, through the gleaming arches, and across rooms that glittered with the treasures of the Linn family. Everywhere were the big, bearded young men who had come from far Europa to conquer an empire about which they could only have heard by hearsay. Looking at them, she felt justified in all the pitiless actions she had taken in her day. They were, it seemed to the grim old woman, living personifications of the chaos that she had fought against all her life.

As she entered the throne room, the darker thoughts faded from her mind. She glanced around with sharp eyes for the mysterious leader. There was no one on or near the throne. Groups of men stood around talking. In one of the groups was a tall, graceful young man, different from all the others in the room. They were bearded. He was clean-shaven.

He saw her and stopped listening to what one of his companions was saying, stopped so noticeably that a silence fell on the group. The silence communicated itself to other groups. After not more than a minute, the roomful of men had faced about and was staring at her, waiting for their commander to speak. Lydia waited, also, examining him swiftly. Czinczar was not a handsome man, but he had an appearance of strength, always a form of good looks. And yet it was not enough. This barbarian world was full of strong-looking men. Lydia, who had expected outstanding qualities, was puzzled.

His face was sensitive rather than brutal, which was unusual. But still not enough to account for the fact that he was absolute lord of an enormous undisciplined horde.

The great man came forward. "Lady," he said, "you have asked to see me."

And then she knew his power. In all her long life she had never heard a baritone voice so resonant, so wonderfully beautiful, so assured of command. It changed him. She realized suddenly that she had been mistaken about his looks. She had sought normal clean-cut handsomeness. This man was beautiful.

The first fear came to her. A voice like that, a personality like that—

She had a vision of this man persuading the Linnan empire to do his will. Mobs hypnotized. The greatest men bewitched. She broke the spell with an effort of will. She said, "You are Czinczar?"

"I am Czinczar."

The definite identification gave Lydia another, though briefer, pause. But this time she recovered more swiftly. And this time, also, her recovery was complete. Her eyes narrowed. She stared at the great man with a developing hostility. "I can see," she said acridly, "that my purpose in coming to see you is going to fail."

"Naturally." Czinczar inclined his head, shrugged. He did not ask her what was her purpose. He seemed incurious. He stood politely, waiting for her to finish what she had to say.

"Until I saw you," said Lydia grimly, "I took it for granted that you were an astute general. Now I see that you consider yourself a man of destiny. I can already see you being lowered into your grave."

There was an angry murmur from the other men in the room. Czinczar waved them into silence. "Madam," he said, "such remarks are offensive to my officers. State your case, and then I will decide what to do with you."

Lydia nodded, but she noted that he did not say that he was offended. She sighed inwardly. She had her mental picture now of this man, and it depressed her. All through known history these natural leaders had been spewed up by the inarticulate masses. They had a will in them to rule or die. But the fact that they frequently died young made no great difference. Their impact on their times was colossal. Such a man could, even in his death throes, drag down long-established dynasties with him. Already, he had killed the legal ruler of Linn and struck a staggering blow at the heart of the empire. By a military freak, it was true—but history accepted such accidents without a qualm.

Lydia said quietly, "I shall be brief since you are no doubt planning high policy and further military campaigns. I have come here at the request of my grandson, Lord Clane Linn."

"The mutation!" Czinczar nodded. His remark was non-committal, an identification, not a comment.

Lydia felt an inward shock that Czinczar's knowledge of the ruling faction should extend to Clane, who had tried to keep himself in the background of Linnan life. She dared not pause to consider the potentialities. She continued quietly. "Lord Clane is a temple scientist, and, as such, he has for many years been engaged in humanitarian scientific experiments. Most of his equipment, unfortunately, is here in Linn." Lydia shrugged. "It is quite valueless to you and your men, but it would be a great loss to civilization if it were destroyed or casually removed. Lord Clane therefore requests that you permit him to send slaves to his town house to remove these scientific instruments to his country estate. In return—"

"Yes," echoed Czinczar, "in return—" His tone was ever so faintly derisive; and Lydia had a sudden realization that he was playing with her. It was not a possibility that she could pay any attention to.

"In return," she said, "he will pay you in precious metals and jewels any reasonable price which you care to name." Having finished, she took a deep breath and waited.

There was a thoughtful expression on the barbarian leader's face. "I have heard," he said, "of Lord Clane's experiments with the so-called"—he hesitated—"god metals of Linn. Very curious stories, some of them; and as soon as I am free from my military duties, I intend to examine this laboratory with my own eyes. You may tell your grandson," he continued with a tone of finality, "that his little scheme to retrieve the greatest treasures in the entire Linnan empire was hopeless from the beginning. Five spaceships descended in the first few minutes of the attack on the estate of Lord Clane to insure that the mysterious weapons there were not used against my invading fleet, and I consider it a great misfortune that he himself was absent in the country at the time. You may tell him that we were not caught by surprise by his midnight attempt two days ago to remove the equipment and that his worst fears as to its fate are justified." He finished, "It is a great relief to know that most of his equipment is safe in our hands."

Lydia said nothing. The phrase, "You may tell him," had had a profound chemical effect on her body.

She hadn't realized she was so tense. It seemed to her that if she spoke she would reveal her own tremendous personal relief. *"You may tell him—"* There could be only one interpretation. She was going to be allowed to depart. Once more she waited.

Czinczar walked forward until he was standing directly in front of her. Something of his barbarous origin, so carefully suppressed until now, came into his manner. A hint of a sneer, the contempt of a physically strong man for decadence, a feeling of genuine basic superiority to the refinement that was in Lydia. When he spoke, he showed that he was consciously aware that he was granting mercy.

"Old woman," he said, "I am letting you go because you did me a great favor when you maneuvered your son, Lord Tews, into the—what did he call it—Lord Advisership. That move, and that alone, gave me the chance I needed to make my attack on the vast Linnan empire." He smiled. "You may depart, bearing that thought in mind."

For some time, Lydia had condemned the sentimental action that had brought Tews into supreme power. But it was a different matter to realize that, far away in interplanetary space, a man had analyzed the move as a major Linnan disaster. She went out without another word.

Czinczar slowly climbed the hill leading up to the low, ugly fence that fronted Lord Clane's town house. He paused at the fence, recognized the temple building material of which it was composed—and then walked on thoughtfully. With the same narrow-eyed interest a few minutes later, he stared at the gushing fountains of boiling water. He beckoned finally to the engineer who had directed the construction of the spaceships that had brought his army to Earth. "How does it work?" he asked.

The designer examined the base of the fountain. He was in no hurry, a big fattish man with a reputation for telling jokes so coarse that strong men winced with shame. He had already set up house in one of the great palaces with three Linnan girls as mistresses and a hundred Linnan men and women as slaves. He was a happy man, with little personal conceit and very little pride as yet to restrain his movements. He located the opening into the fountain and knelt in the dirt like any worker. In that, however, he was not unique. Czinczar knelt beside him, little realizing how his actions shocked the high-born Linnans who belonged to his personal slave retinue. The two men peered into the gloom. "Temple building material," said Meewan, the designer.

Czinczar nodded. They climbed to their feet without further comment, for these were matters that they had discussed at length over a period of years. At the house, a few minutes later, the leader and his henchman both lifted the heavy draperies that covered the walls of a corridor leading into the main laboratory. Like the fence outside, the walls were warm as from some inner heat.

Temple building material! Once again no comment passed between them. They walked on into the laboratory proper; and now they looked at each other in amazement. The room had been noticeably enlarged from its original size, although this they did not know. A great section had been torn out of one wall, and the gap, although it was completely filled in, was still rough and unfinished. But that was only the environment. On almost every square yard of the vast new floor were machines opaque and machines transparent, machines big and small, some apparently complete, others unmistakably mere fragments.

For a moment there was a distinct sense of too much to see. Czinczar walked forward speculatively, glanced at several of the transparent articles with an eye that tried to skim the essentials of shape and inner design. At no time during those first moments did he have any intention of pausing for a detailed examination. And then, out of the corner of his eye he caught a movement.

A glow. He bent down and peered into a long, partly transparent metal case, roughly shaped like a coffin, even as to the colorful and costly-looking lining. The inside, however, curved down to form a narrow channel. Along this channel rolled a ball of light. It turned over sedately, taking approximately one minute to cover the distance to the far side. With the same lack of haste, it paused, seemed to meditate on its next action, and then, with immense deliberation began its return journey.

The very meaningless of the movement fascinated Czinczar. He extended his hand gingerly to within an inch of the ball. Nothing happened. He drew back and pursed his lips. In spite of his attack on Linn, he was not a man who took risks. He beckoned toward a guard. "Bring a slave," he said. Under his direction a former Linnan nobleman, perspiring from every pore, extended his finger and touched the moving ball. His finger went in as if there were nothing there.

He drew back, startled. But the inexorable Czinczar was not through with him. Once more the reluctant, though no longer quite so fearful, finger penetrated the moving ball. The ball rolled into it, through it, beyond it. Czinczar motioned the slave aside and stood looking at him thoughtfully. There must have been something of his purpose in his face, for the man gave a low cry of horror: "Master, I understand nothing of what I have seen. Nothing. Nothing."

"Kill him," said Czinczar.

He turned, scowling, back to the machine. "There must be," he said, and there was a stubborn note in his glorious voice, "some reason for its movements, for—its existence."

Half an hour later he was still examining it.

"If I could only—" thought Clane many times. And knew that he dared not. Not yet.

He had with a certain cynicism permitted the soldiers sent by Lord Tews to remove his equipment to Linn. This included the prize of all his findings, a ball that rolled to and fro in a coffinlike container; a discovery of the golden age that had shaken his certainties to the core of his being.

Because of the ball of energy he had not hesitated to let Tews take control of the artifacts of that ancient and wonderful culture.

He need merely go into the presence of the ball and because of his knowledge of its function could attune himself to it.

It could then be mentally controlled from a distance; all its strange power available—for about three days. At some not precisely determinable time on the third day, it would cease to "come" when he "called" it.

Then he would have to visit it while it was in its container and by direct contact reestablish rapport.

It had seemed evident from Tews' action that the Lord Adviser had not intended to bar him from the equipment. And so the location of the ball in his own Linnan residence under guard had not mattered.

He had not despite his anxieties anticipated a major attack that would capture Linn in one swift assault.

And so the weapon that could end the war was out of his reach, unless he could somehow get to it by cunning means.

He did not yet feel that desperate.

Nor actually were the Linnan forces strong enough to take advantage of a miracle.

Even as in a kind of mental agony he wondered how he would get into Linn, and into his house, he devoted himself to the grim business of training an army as it fought.

There was an old saying in the Linnan army to the effect that, during his first month, a trainee, if put into battle, caused the death of his trained companions. During the second month he hindered retreats made necessary by his presence. And during the third month he was just good enough to get himself killed in the first engagement.

Clane, watching a group of trainees after several weeks of drilling, experienced all the agony of realizing how true the adage was. Learning to fire a bow effectively required complex integration of mind and body. In-fighting with swords had to include the capacity for cooperating with companions. And effective spear fighting was an art in itself.

The plan he outlined that night to the full general staff was an attempt to cover up against the weakness. It was a frank determination to use unfit men as first-line defense troops. He put in a word for the unfit. "Do not overexercise them. Get them out into the open air and simply teach them the first elements of how to use weapons. First, bows and arrows, then spears, and finally swords."

After the meeting, long into the night, he examined reports on the cities of Nouris and Gulf, which had fallen virtually without a fight. As the barbarians attacked, the slaves simply rose up and murdered their masters. A supplementary general-staff report recommended mass execution for all able-bodied male slaves.

The uneasy Clane dispatched messengers to gather commercial and industrial leaders for a morning conference and then unhappily took the slave problem to bed with him.

At ten o'clock he called the meeting to order and told the hundred-odd assembled representative merchants that the army had recommended universal death for male slaves.

His statement caused an immediate uproar.

One man said, "Your excellency, it is impossible. We cannot destroy so much valuable property."

With two exceptions, that seemed to be the attitude. Both exceptions were young men, one of whom said, "Gentlemen, this is a necessary action."

The other said, "My own feeling is that this crisis makes possible a great progressive act—the end of slavery in Linn."

Both men were shouted down by enraged merchants.

Clane stepped forward and raised his hand. When he had silence, he began. "There is no time for half-measures. We must adopt one or the other of these alternatives."

There followed a series of conferences among groups of merchants. Finally a bland spokesman said, "Your excellency, the merchants here present favor *promis*ing the slaves freedom."

For a long moment Clane gazed at his grinning audience, then abruptly turned his back on them and left the room. That afternoon he prepared a special bulletin:

FREEDOM FOR LOYAL SERVANTS

By order of his excellency, Lord Clane Linn, Leader of Linn, temple scientist, beloved of the Atom Gods themselves, it is hereby commanded, and so it shall be forevermore:

GREETINGS to all those good men and women who have quietly and efficiently served the empire in atonement for sins of leaders who rashly led them into hopeless wars against the god-protected Linnan empire— here is the chance of complete freedom that you have earned by your actions and attitudes during the past years.

The empire has been attacked by a cruel and barbarous invader. His reign of terror cannot but be temporary, for invincible forces are gathering against him. An army of a million men is on the way from Mars and Venus, and here on Earth irresistible forces totaling more than two million men are already organizing for battle.

The enemy numbers less than sixty thousand soldiers. To this small army, which gained its initial victory by a surprise and base attack, a few foolish men and women have rashly attached themselves. All the women, unless they are convicted of major crimes, will be spared. For the men who have already gone over to the enemy, there is but one hope: Escape immediately from the barbarian enemy and REPORT TO THE CONCENTRATION CAMPS listed at the bottom of this proclamation. There will be no guards at the camps, but weekly roll calls will be made. And every man whose name appears regularly on these rolls will be granted full freedom when the enemy is defeated.

For hardened recalcitrants the penalty is death.

To those men and women still loyally serving at their appointed tasks, I, Lord Clane, acting Lord Leader of Linn, give the following commands:

All women and children will remain at their present residences, continuing to serve as in the past.

All men report to their masters and say, "It is my intention to take advantage of the offer of Lord Clane. Give me a week's food so that I, too, may report to a concentration camp."

Having done this, and having received the food, leave at once. DO NOT DELAY A SINGLE HOUR.

If for some reason your master is not at home, take the food and go without permission. No one will hinder you in your departure from the city.

Any man to whom this order applies who is found lurking within any city or town twenty-four hours after this proclamation is posted will be suspected of treasonable intent.

The penalty is death.

Any man who after one week is found within a fifty-mile radius of a city will be suspected of treasonable intent.

The penalty is death.

To save yourself, go to a concentration camp and appear regularly for roll call. If the barbarians attack your camp, scatter into the forests and hills and hide, or go to another camp. Adequate food rations will be supplied all camps.

All those of proven loyalty will receive freedom when the war is over. They will immediately have the right to marry. Settlement land will be opened up. After five years citizenship rights, granted alien immigrants, will be available on application.

This is the end of slavery in the Linnan empire.

BE WISE—BE SAFE—BE FREE

It was a document that had its weak points. Before issuing it, Clane spent time arguing its merits to a group of doubtful officers—he ignored the merchants; they were too venal to be considered. He pointed out that it would be impossible to keep secret a general order for mass execution. A majority of the slaves would escape, and then they would really be dangerous. He admitted that the proclamation, though he meant every word of the promise in it, was full of lies. A million slaves in Linn alone had gone over to Czinczar, many of them trained soldiers. Czinczar could use them to garrison any city he might capture and thus have his own army free for battle. It was Morkid, sardonic and scathing, who ended the argument late in the afternoon.

"Gentlemen," he said, "you do not seem to be aware that our commander-in-chief has at one stroke cut through all our illusions and false hopes, and penetrated straight to the roots of the situation in which we find ourselves. What is clear by the very nature of our discussion is that we have no choice." His voice went up. "In this period when disaster is so imminent, we are fortunate in having as our leader a genius of the first rank who has already set us on the only military path that can lead to victory.

"Gentlemen"—his voice rang with the tribute—"I give you Lord Clane Linn, acting Lord Leader of Linn."

The clapping lasted for five minutes.

Clane watched the battle for Goram from a patrol craft that darted from strong point to strong point. Enemy squadrons tried again and again to close in on him, but his own machine was faster and more maneuverable.

The familiar trick of getting above him was tried, an old device in patrol craft and spaceship fighting. But the expected energy flow upward did not take place. His small vessel did not even sag, which was normally the minimum reaction when two sources of atomic energy operated on a gravity line.

The efforts worried Clane. Czinczar was, of course, aware by this time that his enemy knew more about the metals of the gods than he or his technicians. But it would be unfortunate if they should conclude from the actions of this one ship that Clane himself was inside. He wanted to see this battle. In spite of everything, minute by minute, he saw it.

The defense was tough, tougher than he had anticipated from the fact that four more cities had fallen in the past four weeks. The untrained were fighting grimly for their lives. Arrows took a toll of the attackers. Spears, awkwardly but desperately manipulated, inflicted wounds and sometimes death. The sword-fighting stage was the worst. The muscular and powerful barbarians, once they penetrated the weapons that could attack them from a distance, made short work of their weaker adversaries.

The first line was down, devastated, defeated. The second-line battle began. Barbarian reserves came forward and were met by waves of arrows that darkened the sky—and took their toll when they struck the advancing groups of men. Hoarse cries of pain, curses, the shrieks of the desperately wounded, the agonized horror of Linnans suddenly cut off and doomed, rose up to the ears of those in the darting small craft. The defenders strove to stay together. That was part of their instructions. Retreat slowly to the central squares—which were strongly held against a surprise rear attack.

Retreat, and at the last minute spaceships would land and rescue the hard-pressed, but theoretically still intact army of what had once been able-bodied civilians. After a month and a half of training they were too valuable to sacrifice in a last-ditch fight.

As it was, their dogged resistance was shaping the pattern of the war. Surely, Czinczar, counting his men after each battle, must already be having his own private doubts. His army as a whole, augmented by the unrepentant among the slaves, was increasing daily. But the larger the army grew, the smaller was his chance of controlling it.

Yet there was no doubt about this battle, or this city. As the dark tide of night slipped in from the east, victory fires began to burn in all the important streets. The smoke wreathed into the sky, and blood-red flames licked up into the blackness. The Linnans below, at this very moment enduring the beginning of a barbarian occupation, would not be in a humor to appreciate that their grudgingly accepted defeat represented a possible turning point in the war.

The time had come to decide when and where and under what conditions the main Linnan force would be thrown into a decisive battle for the control of the planet. And there was another decision, also, involving an immensely risky attempt to get near the ball of light. Clane shifted uneasily and drew his cloak tightly around his thin shoulders.

He was still considering ways and means when a message was brought him by a released Linnan nobleman who had been captured by the barbarians.

The message was a one-sentence question from Czinczar. "Have you ever wondered, my dear Lord Clane, how the civilization of the golden age was so *completely* destroyed?"

It was a problem about which Clane had pondered many times. But it had never occurred to him that the answer might be known to a barbarian from a remote moon of Jupiter.

He questioned the released nobleman, a middle-aged knight of the empire, as to conditions in Linn. The answers were not pleasant. Many slaves had taken revenge on their former masters. Numerous Linnan women of rank had been reduced to the status of prostitute.

In questioning the man for any news of his Linnan residence, he learned that Czinczar had publicly invited temple scientists to take care of "certain relics" formerly in the possession of Lord Clane.

Clane said at that point, "He actually mentioned my name."

"It was posted," was the reply, and the man shrugged.

"I read it on one of my errands out of the palace grounds."

Long after the interview was over, Clane considered that. He suspected a trap—and yet Czinczar could not know how immensely valuable that sphere was.

If the barbarian leader had looked into it through a hollow tube, he might be startled at what was "inside." But still it would do him no good.

Nevertheless, suppose it was a trap.

It still made no difference. For his purpose, momentary proximity to the ball was all that would be required. Dared he take the chance?

He was still considering the gamble when another released nobleman brought a second message from Czinczar:

> I shall like to have a conversation with you and should like to show you an object the like of which—I'll wager—you have never seen. Can you think of a way in which such a meeting could be arranged?

Lord Clane showed the message to the general staff at its meeting the following morning. They unanimously forbade such a rendezvous but agreed that it was an opportunity to send a formal message to the barbarian leader.

The mutation, who had his own reasons for appearing firm, had already written the communication. He read it to the assembled officers:

> To the barbarian chieftain, Czinczar:
> Your cowardly attempt to win mercy for your crimes against humanity by a personal appeal to myself is of no avail. Get off this planet with your barbarous forces. Only immediate compliance can save you and Europa from destruction. Take heed!
>
> Clane,
> Acting Lord Leader

The message was approved and dispatched in the care of a captured barbarian officer. Clane began immediately to complete preparations for launching an attack against the city of Linn. Such an attack had been discussed several times by the staff and had been agreed on reluctantly, as a feint. The generals felt that a landing might confuse the defenders of the city and thus enable the Linnan army to recapture key outlying cities, which would indeed be the real goal. It was understood that the assault force would withdraw from Linn during the night of the day of attack.

Clane was content with this. He set out for the city of Linn the day before the attack, making the initial part of the journey in an air scooter. From this, in a secluded spot, he unloaded a donkey and a cart of vegetables, and trudged beside it the final twelve miles.

In his drab work garb of a temple initiate, he was one of many carts; and at no time was there any problem. So vast was the slave army that held Linn that Czinczar's forces had quickly sought to establish a normal flow of food from the surrounding countryside into the city to ward off starvation.

Linnan scouts had long since reported that the gates were open.

Clane entered without interference from the former slaves who guarded that particular gate. Once inside, he was even less conspicuous, and no one questioned his right to go along the street toward his city residence. He climbed the hill at the trades entrance and was permitted to take his cart through an opening in the low fence by the single barbarian soldier who guarded that section of it.

Dutifully, as if he were sent on lawful business, he headed for the trades entrance of the house, and he turned the vegetables over to two women and said, "Who is in charge today?"

He was given a barbarian name. "Gleedon!"

"Where is he?" Clane asked.

"In the office, of course—through there." The older woman pointed along the main hallway, which led through the large central room where most of the precious machinery and equipment had been stored.

As he entered the great room, he saw that there were a dozen barbarian soldiers at the various entrances. He saw also that the container with the ball of light was at the center of the chamber.

. . . Misty sphere, vaguely glowing as if from an inner flame, rolling to and fro . . .

He could walk by and touch it in passing.

Without appearing too hurried, he walked forward, put

his finger through the flimsy surface of the sphere, and, without pausing, continued on toward the office.

He was sorely tempted, at this point, to take no further chances. If he acted at once and seized the house, then he would have control of the box.

But if he carried through with his original plan and then the box were removed so that he could not find it during the three days that the sphere would not be activated— He shuddered and refused to think of such an eventuality.

He had been impressed by Czinczar's communications. The barbarian leader had important information to give. Somehow, somewhere, he had gotten hold of an object so valuable that he had risked his self-esteem in attempting to establish contact.

If too hasty action were taken, that knowledge might be lost.

Even as he walked on through the room, the mutation silently reaffirmed his purpose. A moment later he entered the office and informed the barbarian officer there that he had come for the job of taking care of the relics of the atom gods.

The big man stood up and squinted down at him, gave an almost naïve start of recognition, and then called two soldiers from the hallway.

And then he said, "Lord Clane Linn, you are under arrest."

To one of the soldiers he commanded, "Get ropes. Tie him up."

Meekly, the mutation submitted to being bound.

The moment the news arrived, Czinczar headed for Linn. He was met on the roof of the central palace by Meewan. The big man had a smile on his plump, good-fellow face. "Your theory was right," he said admiringly. "You thought he would take a chance at the critical period of the invasion. He arrived this morning."

"Tell me exactly how you accepted his services." The golden voice spoke softly. The strange face was thoughtful as the other man gave his detailed account. There seemed no end to his interest. When the story was finished, he asked question after question. Each answer seemed merely to stimulate new questions. Meewan said finally, querulous-ly:

"Your excellency, I have no doubt that our men have put the best face on the capture to make themselves look good. They claim to have captured him as he entered the building, before he could do anything or touch anything. Since they're a lax bunch of rascals, I question this. But what does it matter? What are you doubtful about?"

That gave Czinczar pause; he had not realized how tense he was. After all, he told himself, the situation was simple enough. He had issued an open invitation for temple scientists to come and take care of "some god-metal relics" that had fallen into possession of the conquerors. It was a cleverly worded request, designed to win general approval from the defeated even as it drew *the* temple scientist to his own undoing. Its only stipulation, very guardedly worded, was that in return for the privilege of sharing the "safe-guarding of the relics," experiments should be continued as if no war were being waged.

"The gods," Czinczar had said sanctimoniously in the invitation, "are above the petty quarrels of mankind."

Apparently, at least one of its purposes was accomplished. The mutation himself had applied for the job. Czinczar meditated cautiously on tactics. "Bring him here," he said finally. "We can't take any risks of his having established control over anything at his house. We know too little and he too much."

While he waited, he examined the rod of force—which was one of the few workable instruments that had been found in the house. He was not a man who accepted past truths as final. That it had worked a week ago did not mean that it would work now. He tested it from a great window, pointing it at the upper foliage of a nearby tree. No sound, no visible light spewed forth—but the upper section of the tree crashed down onto a pathway below. Czinczar experienced the satisfaction of a logical man whose logic had proved correct. It was not an uncommon satisfaction. From the early days when he had been a back-country transcriber of messages to the days of his rise to power, he had taken risks that seemed necessary, no more, no less. Even now he could not be sure that the atomic wizard, Lord Clane, would not defeat him by some decisive

71

wile. For several minutes, he pondered that and then ordered a box brought in from the ice room of the palace. The contents of the box had come all the way from Europa packed in ice. He was indicating to the slaves where to place the box when an officer burst breathlessly into the throne room.

"Excellency," he cried. "Hundreds of spaceships. It's an attack."

Standing at the windows a moment later, watching the ships settling down, Czinczar realized that his hazy suspicions had been correct. The appearance of Clane in the city was part of a planned maneuver that would now run its deadly course. It was a pleasure to know that Lord Clane himself was caught in a trap.

He wasted no time watching a battle that he could not hope to see from the palace in any important detail. Nor did he have the feeling Tews had had months earlier that it was necessary for commanders to know where he was in the early stages of the engagement. He issued quick instructions, ordering the ice-packed box sent after him, and wrote a note for Meewan. Then he rode with a strong escort to the headquarters of the reserve army in the middle of the city.

The reserve contained a barbarian core, but like the main defense of the city it was overwhelmingly made up of slaves. Czinczar's arrival was greeted by a roar of excitement. The cheers did not die down until long after he had entered the building.

He talked over the situation with some of the slave officers and found them calm and confident. According to their estimates sixty thousand Linnan soldiers had landed in the first wave. That that was exactly the number of barbarians who had originally invaded the city did not seem to occur to the slaves. But the comparison struck Czinczar sharply. He wondered if it was designed to have some symbolic meaning. The possibility made him sardonic. Not symbols but swords spoke the language of victory.

As the afternoon dragged on, the Linnan attack was being held everywhere. The box, still dripping, was delivered from the palace about three. Since there was no longer any immediate danger, Czinczar sent a messenger to Meewan. At three-thirty Meewan came in grinning broadly. He was followed by slave Linnans carrying a sedan chair. In the chair, bound hand and foot, was the acting Lord Leader of Linn. There was complete silence as the chair was set down, and the slaves withdrew.

Clane studied the barbarian leader with genuine interest. Lady Lydia's opinion of the man had impressed him more than he cared to admit. The question was, could this strong, fine-looking military genius be panicked into thinking that the atom gods existed? Panicked now, during the next half hour? Fortunately, for the first time in his career as an atomic scientist, he had behind him the greatest power ever developed by the wizards of the fabulous days of the legends. He saw that the impersonal expression on the other's face was transforming into the beginning of contempt.

"By the god pits," said Czinczar in disgust, "you Linnans are all the same—weaklings every one."

Clane said nothing. He had looked often with regret into mirrors that showed him exactly what Czinczar was seeing. A slim, young man with a face that was white and woman-ish and . . . well, it couldn't be helped.

Czinczar's face changed again. There was suddenly irony in it. "I am speaking," he asked politely, "to Lord Clane Linn? We have not made a mistake?"

Clane couldn't let the opening pass. "No mistake," he said quietly. "I came into Linn for the sole purpose of talking to you while the battle was on. And here I am."

It must have sounded ridiculous, coming from a man bound as he was. The near guards guffawed, and Meewan giggled. Only Czinczar showed no sign. And his marvelous voice was as steady as steel as he said, "I have not the time to flirt with words, nor the inclination. I can see that you are counting on something to save you, and I presume it has something to do with your knowledge of atomic energy."

He fingered the rod of force suggestively. "So far as I can see, we can kill you in less than a second whenever we desire."

Clane shook his head. "You are in error. It is quite impossible for you to kill me."

There was a sound from Meewan. The engineer came forward. "Czinczar," he said darkly, "this man is intolerable.

Give me permission to slap his face, and we shall see if his atom gods protect him from indignity."

Czinczar waved him aside. But he stared down at the prisoner with eyes that were abnormally bright. The swiftness with which tension had come into the room amazed him. And, incredibly, it was the prisoner who had seized the advantage— "Impossible to kill me!" In one sentence he dared them to make the attempt.

There was a crinkle of frown in Czinczar's forehead. He had been careful in his handling of Clane as a matter of common sense, not because he actually anticipated disaster. But now, quite frankly, he admitted to himself that the man was not reacting normally. The words Clane had spoken had a ring in them, a conviction that could no longer be ignored. The purpose of his own invasion of the Linnan empire could be in danger.

He said urgently, "I have something to show you. No attempt will be made to kill you until you have seen it. For your part, do nothing hasty, take no action, whatever power you have, until you have gazed with understanding."

He was aware of Meewan's giving him an astounded glance.

"Power!" exclaimed the designer, and it was like a curse. "The power *he* has!"

Czinczar paid no attention. This was his own special secret, and there could be no delay.

"Guards," he said, "bring the box over here."

It was soaking wet when they brought it. It left a dirty trail of water on the priceless rug, and a pool began to accumulate immediately in the place where it was set down. There was a delay while sweating men pried off the top. Even the guards at far doors strained to see the contents. A gasp of horror broke the tension of waiting.

What was inside was about eight feet long. Its width was indeterminable, for it seemed to have folds in its body that gave an impression of great size. It had obviously died only a short time before it was packed in ice. It looked fresh, almost alive, there in its case of ice, unhuman, staring with sightless eyes at the ornate ceiling.

"Where did you get it?" Clane asked at last.

"It was found on one of the moons—within hours after a strange ship was sighted."

74

"How long ago?" The mutation spoke in a steady tone.

"Two years, Earth time."

"It would seem that whoever was in the ship will have departed by now."

Czinczar shook his head. "Miners found a second body exactly like this on a meteorite in a spacesuit—seven months ago."

For a long time the mutation gazed down at the creature. Finally he looked, and his eyes met Czinczar's waiting gaze. He said slowly, "What is your theory?"

"A nonhuman race of great scientific attainments. Ruthless, unfriendly—for there are reports of sudden destruction in outlying areas of Europa which puzzled me until this body was found . . . I tend to wonder if this might not be a second visitation to the solar system. I cannot give you briefly all the logical relationships I have visualized, but my feeling is that the civilization of the golden age was destroyed by the first visitation."

Clane said, "I am glad that you have shown me this, but what is your purpose in doing so?"

Czinczar drew a deep breath. And made his second move to avert the catastrophe suggested by every action and manner of this unorthodox prisoner. He said, "It would be a grave error for either of us to destroy each other's armies."

"You are asking for mercy?"

That was too strong to take. The barbarian showed his teeth in a snarl. "I am asking for common sense," he said.

"It's impossible," said Clane. "The people must have their revenge. In victory they will accept nothing less than your death."

The words brought an obscene curse from Meewan. "Czinczar," he shouted, "what is all this nonsense? I have never seen you like this. I follow no man who accepts defeat in advance. I'll show you what we'll do with this . . . this—" He broke off, "Guards, put a spear into him."

Nobody moved. The soldiers looked uneasily at Czinczar, who nodded coolly. "Go right ahead," he said. "If he can be killed, I'd like to know."

Still nobody moved. It was apparently too mild an order, or something of the leader's tension had communicated to the men. They looked at each other, and they were standing there doubtfully when Meewan snatched a sword from one of them and turned toward the bound man.

That was as far as he got. Where he had been was a ball of light.

"Try," came the voice of Clane, "to use the rod of force against me." A fateful pause. "Try. It won't kill you."

Czinczar raised the rod of force and pressed the activator. Nothing happened— Wait! The ball of light was growing brighter.

Clane's voice split the silence tantalizingly. "Do you still not believe in the gods?"

"I am astonished," said Czinczar, "that you do not fear the spread of superstition more than the spread of knowledge. We so-called barbarians," he said proudly, "despise you for your attempt to fence in the human spirit. We are freethinkers, and all your atomic energy will fail in the end to imprison us."

He shrugged. "As for your control over that ball, I do not pretend to understand it."

At last, he had shocked the mutation out of his ice-cold manner. "You actually," said Clane incredulously, "do not believe in the atom gods?"

"Guards," shouted Czinczar piercingly, "attack him from every side."

The ball of light flickered but did not seem to move. There were no guards.

"Now do you believe?" Clane asked.

The barbarian looked haggard and old. But he shook his head. "I have lost the war," he mumbled. "Only that I recognize. It is up to you to take up the mantle which has fallen from my shoulders." He broke off. "What in the name of your gods is that ball?"

"It contains the entire sidereal universe."

Czinczar knit his brow and leaned forward as if he were trying to understand.

"The what universe?" he asked at last.

"When you look inside through a hollow tube," Clane explained patiently, "you see stars. It's like a window into space—only it's not a window. It's the universe itself."

The barbarian leader looked genuinely bewildered. "This universe?" he said blankly.

Clane nodded but made no comment. It hadn't been easy

to grasp so vast an idea, even with the written explanations that he had found.

Czinczar shook his head. "You mean the Earth is in there?" He pointed at the glowing sphere.

"It's a fourth-dimensional idea," said Clane; and still he remained patient. He could recognize a bemused man when he saw one. It was not the moment to press any other point.

The barbarian narrowed his eyes and said at last, "How can you get a large object into a smaller one?" His tone appealed for a logical explanation.

Clane shrugged. "When largeness or smallness are illusions of viewpoints, the problem does not exist."

Czinczar scowled at that and straightened. "I have been assuming," he said, "that at this point in our relations you would be speaking nothing but truth. Evidently, you are not prepared to tell me anything valid about your weapon. Naturally, I reject this fanciful story."

Clane shook his head but said nothing. He had given the only explanation he had, and it had run up against the other man's magnificent realism. Not that he blamed the barbarian. Only gradually had he himself been able to accept the idea that matter and energy were different than they appeared to the sense perceptions of the body.

But now it was time to act, to force, to convince. The bonds fell from him as if they did not exist. He stood up, and now that crown among all the jewels of the ages rode above his head in a matchless perfect rhythm with his movements.

Czinczar said stubbornly, "It would be a mistake to kill any able-bodied man, slave or otherwise."

Clane said, "The gods demand absolute surrender."

Czinczar said in fury, "You fool, I am offering you the solar system! Has this monster in the box not changed your mind in the slightest degree?"

"It has."

"But then—"

"I do not," said Clane, "believe in joint-leadership arrangements."

A pause. Then Czinczar said, "You have come far—who once used atomic power merely to stay alive."

"Yes," said Clane, "I have come far."

Czinczar frowned down at the thing in the box. "The real threat to Linn is there. Will you promise to try for the Lord Leadership?"

"I," Clane said, "can promise nothing."

They looked at each other, two men who almost understood each other. It was Czinczar who broke the silence. "I make an absolute surrender," he said and it was a sigh, "to you and you alone, of all my forces—in the belief that you have the courage and common sense to shirk none of your new duties as Protector of the Solar System. It was a role," he finished somewhat unnecessarily, suddenly gloomy, "that I originally intended for myself."

In a well-guarded room in a remote suburb of Linn a core of energy rolled sedately back and forth along a narrow path. In all the solar system there was nothing else like that core. It looked small, but that was an illusion of man's senses. The books that described it and the men who had written the books knew but a part of its secrets.

They knew that the micro-universe inside it pulsed with a multiform of minus forces. It reacted to cosmic rays and atomic energy like some insatiable sponge. No submolecular energy released in its presence could escape it. And the moment it reached its own strange variation of critical mass it could start a meson chain reaction in anything it touched.

One weakness it had, and men had seized upon that in their own greedy fashion. It imitated thought. Or so it seemed. *So it seemed.*

The great question that Clane, and before him the ancients, asked after observing this remarkable characteristic was: Did this mean that . . . man controlled the universe or that the universe controlled man?

ERSATZ ETERNAL

GRAYSON REMOVED THE IRONS from the other's wrists and legs. "Hart!" he said sharply.

The young man on the cot did not stir. Grayson hesitated and then deliberately kicked the man. "Damn you, Hart, listen to me! I'm releasing you—just in case I don't come back."

John Hart neither opened his eyes nor showed any awareness of the blow he had received. He lay inert; and the only evidence of life in him was that he was limp, not rigid. There was almost no color in his cheeks. His black hair was damp and stringy.

Grayson said earnestly, "Hart, I'm going out to look for Malkins. Remember, he left four days ago, intending only to be gone twenty-four hours."

When there was no response, the older man started to turn away, but he hesitated and said, "Hart, if I don't come back, you must realize where we are. This is a new planet, understand. We've never been here before. Our ship was wrecked, and the three of us came down in a lifeboat, and what we need is fuel. That's what Malkins went out to look for, and now I'm going out to look for Malkins."

The figure on the cot remained blank. And Grayson walked reluctantly out the door and off toward the hills. He had no particular hope.

Three men were down on a planet God-only-knew-where —and one of those men was violently insane.

As he walked along, he glanced around him in occasional puzzlement. The scenery was very earthlike: trees, shrubs, grass, and distant mountains misted by blue haze. It was still a little odd that when they had landed Malkins and he had had the distinct impression that they were coming down onto a barren world without atmosphere and without life.

A soft breeze touched his cheeks. The scent of flowers was in the air. He saw birds flitting among the trees, and once he heard a song that was startlingly like that of a meadow lark.

He walked all day and saw no sign of Malkins. Nor was there any habitation to indicate that the planet had intelligent life. Just before dusk he heard a woman calling his name.

Grayson turned with a start, and it was his mother, looking much younger than he remembered her in her coffin eight years before. She came up, and she said severely, "Billie, don't forget your rubbers."

Grayson stared at her with eyes that kept twisting away in disbelief. Then, deliberately, he walked over and touched her. She caught his hand, and her fingers were warm and lifelike.

She said, "I want you to go tell your father that dinner is ready."

Grayson released himself and stepped back, and looked tensely around him. The two of them stood on an empty, grassy plain. Far in the distance was the gleam of a silver-shining river.

He turned away from her and strode on into the twilight. When he looked back, there was no one in sight. But presently a boy was moving in step beside him. Grayson paid no attention at first, but presently he stole a glance at his companion.

It was himself at the age of fifteen.

Just before the gathering night blotted out any chance of recognition, he saw that a second boy was now striding along beside the first. Himself, aged about eleven.

Three Bill Graysons, thought Grayson. He began to laugh wildly.

Then he began to run. When he looked back, he was alone. Sobbing under his breath, he slowed to a walk, and almost immediately heard the laughter of children in the soft darkness. Familiar sounds, yet the impact of them was stunning.

Grayson babbled at them, "All me, at different ages. Get away! I know you're only hallucinations."

When he had worn himself out, when there was nothing left to his voice but a harsh whisper, he thought, *Only hallucinations? Am I sure?*

He felt unutterably depressed and exhausted. "Hart and me," he said aloud, wearily, "we belong in the same asylum."

Dawn came, cool; and his hope was that sunrise would bring an end to the madness of the night. As the slow light lengthened over the land, Grayson looked around him in bewilderment. He was on a hill, and below him spread his home town of Calypso, Ohio.

He stared down at it with unbelieving eyes, and then, because it looked as real as life, he started to run toward it.

It *was* Calypso, but as it had been when he was a boy. He headed for his own house. And there he was; he'd know that boy of ten anywhere. He called out to the youngster, who took one look at him, turned away, and ran into the house.

Grayson lay down on the lawn, and covered his eyes. "Someone," he told himself, "some*thing*—is taking pictures out of my mind and making me see them."

It seemed to him that if he hoped to remain sane—and alive—he'd have to hold that thought.

It was the sixth day after Grayson's departure. Aboard the lifeboat, John Hart stirred and opened his eyes. "Hungry," he said aloud to no one in particular.

He waited he knew not for what and then wearily sat up, slipped off the cot, and made his way to the galley. When he had eaten, he walked to the lock-door, and stood for a long time staring out over the earthlike scene that spread before him. It made him feel better, vaguely.

He jumped abruptly down to the ground and began to walk toward the nearest hilltop. Darkness was falling rapidly, but it did not occur to him to turn back.

Soon the ship was lost in the night behind him.

A girlfriend of his youth was the first to talk to him. She came out of the blackness; and they had a long conversation.

In the end they decided to marry.

The ceremony was immediately completed by a minister who drove up in a car and found both families assembled in a beautiful home in the suburbs of Pittsburgh. The clergyman was an old man whom Hart had known in his childhood.

The young couple went to New York City and to Niagara Falls for their honeymoon, then headed by aero-taxi for California to make their home. Suddenly there were three children, and they owned a hundred-thousand-acre ranch with a million cattle on it, and there were cowboys who dressed like movie stars.

For Grayson, the civilization that sprang into full-grown existence around him on what had originally been a barren, airless planet had nightmarish qualities. The people he met had a life expectancy of less than seventy years. Children were born in nine months and ten days after conception.

He buried six generations of one family that he had founded. And then, one day as he was crossing Broadway—in New York City—the small sturdiness, the walk, and the manner of a man coming from the opposite direction made him stop short.

"Henry!" he shouted. "Henry Malkins!"

"Well, I'll be—Bill Grayson."

They shook hands, silent after the first excited greeting. Malkins spoke first. "There's a bar around the corner."

During the middle of the second drink John Hart's name came up.

"A life force, seeking form, used his mind," said Grayson matter-of-factly. "It apparently has no expression of its own. It tried to use me—" He glanced at Malkins questioningly.

The other man nodded. "And me!" he said.

"I guess we resisted too hard."

Malkins wiped the perspiration from his forehead. "Bill," he said, "it's all like a dream. I get married and divorced every forty years. I marry what seems to be a twenty-year-old girl. In a few decades she looks five hundred."

"Do you think it's all in our minds?"

"No, no—nothing like that. I think all this civilization exists—whatever I mean by existence." Malkins groaned. "Let's not get into that. When I read some of the philosophy explaining life, I feel as if I'm on the edge of an abyss. If only we could get rid of Hart, somehow."

Grayson was smiling grimly. "So you haven't found out yet?"

"What do you mean?"

"Have you got a weapon on you?"

Silently, Malkins produced a needle-beam projector. Grayson took it, pointed it at his own right temple, and pressed the curved firing pin—as Malkins grabbed at him frantically but too late.

The thin, white beam seemed to penetrate Grayson's head. It burned a round, black, smoldering hole in the woodwork beyond. Coolly, the unhurt Grayson pointed the triangular muzzle at his companion.

"Like me to try it on you?" he asked jovially.

The older man shuddered and grabbed at the weapon. "Give me that!" he said.

He calmed presently and asked, "I've noticed that I'm no older. Bill, what are we going to do?"

"I think we're being held in reserve," said Grayson.

He stood up and held out his hand. "Well, Henry, it's been good seeing you. Suppose we meet here every year from now on and compare notes."

"But—"

Grayson smiled a little tautly. "Brace up, my friend. Don't you see? This is the biggest thing in the universe. We're going to live forever. We're possible substitutes if anything goes wrong."

"But what is it? What's doing it?"

"Ask me a million years from now. Maybe I'll have an answer."

He turned and walked out of the bar. He did not look back.

THE SOUND OF
WILD LAUGHTER

CHAPTER I

WHEN THE NEWS came of her husband's accident, there flashed into Marie's mind an aphorism of his that had always offended her at least as much as any of his other obnoxious ideas: "The first reaction of the wife of a modern male when he passes on is relief. Today, every woman feels that she has married the wrong man and that she will now get a better one—"

There was more to the saying. But she had always been convinced that in writing that portion and repeatedly quoting it to her, Carl had wanted to control how she would feel if it ever happened.

Standing there in her parents' home after she had replaced the receiver, Marie couldn't quite believe that he was seriously hurt. Not that supreme cynic!

Co-winner—with herself—of the Nobel Prize in physics the previous year, head of his own manufacturing laboratory, president of the Non-Pareil Corporation, self-reported lover of dozens of women, author of an extremely mechanistic philosophy of feminine behavior, each comment of which was written in his own hand in an unpublished book titled: *Women Are Doomed*—the Aphorisms of Dr. Carl Hazzard . . . somehow he had never seemed vulnerable.

Later, as she was preparing to fly to New York before proceeding to the West Coast, another phone call came with additional news. Dr. Angus MacKerrie, chief surgeon of the Brain Study Foundation, had operated and successfully removed Carl's brain a few minutes before death came to his shattered body.

Startled, Marie remembered.

Carl and she, and many other scientists, had a few years before signed an agreement with the Foundation, donating their brains. The purpose was to keep the thinking ability alive after death.

Marie had no clear idea how she should feel. Certainly not grief.

A third phone call—from Dr. Walter Drexel—speaking in a strangely tense voice, was brief. He obtained her flight schedule and said, "Marie, I know this will sound strange to you, but I'll meet you in New York. It's very important."

He was there at the airfield, tall, well-dressed, serious, a good-looking man in his early forties.

He had, he said, rented a room for her in a small, luxurious hotel on East 48th Street, and he had reserved a table at an exclusive restaurant nearby. It was all very odd indeed, but Walter had been chief physicist at the Hazzard Laboratories, and in the natural course of things he might now be elevated to Carl's position. Marie went in the taxi with him, puzzled but not disturbed.

It was a very private dinner in a booth. As soon as their cocktails were served, Walter began in a low voice. "After you left—at Carl's suggestion, I understand?—"

She nodded. "He wanted me to visit my parents."

"He called me into his office. He told me that he had seen a look pass between you and me that instantly apprised him that we were having an affair."

Something inside Marie sagged. The old shame. She said, distressed, "Don't worry, Walter, I've been through this before."

Walter continued. "He gave me a week's notice. He said he would have fired me except that he didn't wish to arouse anyone's suspicion that I was being discharged because of you. He said he didn't want your reputation tarnished. He told me to figure out some face-saving reason for leaving."

Marie said, "You're reinstated as of right now."

"Thanks, Marie." The physicist was grave. "But if that

was what all this was about, I'd have stayed in Los Angeles and told it to you there. I imagine he thought he was digging the knife into your lover because he told me that he would tell the papers of your numerous other affairs of the heart, describe to the world what a nightmare existence he's been living as the husband of a loose woman—"

"That philanderer said *that!*"

The outrageous reversal of truth left Marie momentarily in a rage but not surprised. In the very first year of their marriage Carl had let her know that he had a mistress, or two, or three. She had promptly moved down the hall into her own apartment. Shortly after, Carl had expressed his first suspicion of *her* with what was probably his initial aphorism: "The term 'good' woman is a misnomer. Every human female has backed herself into some psychologically secure corner. Being 'good' is merely one of these corners, though it must be one of the safer ones because a majority of American women are using it as their base of operations."

Carl had contended that her outward appearance of frigidity was merely an aspect of "cornering."

She found her voice. "Surely you let him know that you were innocent."

Walter replied earnestly, "Marie, it was like talking to a demented person. As he said these things about you, those black eyes of his were bright and glistening, his lips trembled, and there were beads of perspiration on his high cheekbones—"

It was a vivid picture of a Carl that Marie knew well. She said, "He was undoubtedly entering one of his periodic jealous phases. In the past he would hire a detective and have me followed. On occasion I'd find him in my room, sniffing. He told me he could smell the presence of a man —a lie because there never was any. His shrewdest aphorisms came from these times—"

She stopped. The old feeling of utter disgust came over her.

Walter said, "Marie, this brain operation changes everything. Do you realize that the Brain Study Foundation expects to communicate with Carl as soon as the anesthetic wears off?"

Marie hadn't thought about it at all.

She sat now, realizing, remembering the months during which Carl's and her brain waves had been recorded and correlated with the way they spoke. Every syllable and sound they made had been transformed into analogs for installation in a computer.

Walter went on in a gray voice. "Marie, if Carl comes to and is still in this jealous state of extreme suspicion, he may say something against us."

Marie sat frozen with fear. It would take only a single accusation to ruin Walter's and her reputation.

Walter finished in a desperate tone. "Marie, you're his wife. Wire the Foundation to delay any attempts at communication till we get there. You and I have got to talk to Carl first. Use all your legal rights, no matter what anyone thinks."

"But we signed releases," she whispered, "which—"

"You've got to!" His voice was hoarse. "There's no alternative."

With a hand that trembled, he took two telegram forms from his inside breast pocket. "This one's for your attorney —what's his name?"

"Bob Lindley." She corrected, "Carl's attorney."

"Your attorney now," said Walter. "And this other one is to Dr. MacKerrie at the Foundation."

He read the messages to her. They were substantially the same. One urged the attorney to negotiate at once with the Foundation, denying them any communication with Carl without her express permission. The other made the same urgent request of MacKerrie.

Mention of Dr. MacKerrie reminded Marie that it was he who had made the numerous encephalographic recordings of Carl's brain waves and her own. He remembered something else. Carl had always felt that "Mac" had stayed around longer than was necessary because, as he had put it in his mechanistic fashion, "His libido senses that there's an unused woman around here, meaning you, my sweet."

Another saying of Carl's flitted through her mind. "When a woman discovers that a man loves her, she has a strong impulse to make use of him. This is not always wise."

But the tense hope was in her now: "If Carl was right; if Mac really fell for me . . . he will persuade the others—"

Aloud, in a steady voice, she said, "Tell them which plane we'll be on tomorrow—and send the telegrams!"

Walter corrected: "Which plane *you'll* be on. Let's not get anyone suspecting *me!*"

He sped eagerly out to the lobby to send the messages.

Chapter II

Morning.

The big jet was an hour out from New York when the first answering telegram was handed to Marie. She read:

TOO LATE TO STOP INITIAL INTERVIEW. AL-READY RELEASED TO TV AND RADIO. FOUNDA-TION PROMISES COMPLETE COOPERATION IN FUTURE. LOVE, MAC.

Marie was aware of Walter leaning over from the ad-joining seat, straining to read. She thrust the telegram into his hands, whispering, "It doesn't sound as if Carl made any accusation."

She had a strong sense of relief, the feeling that a crisis had been avoided.

She grew aware that Walter was writing furiously on the back of the telegram. As he pushed the paper into her hands, she saw that his pupils were dilated and his features contorted. He whispered:

"Marie, you've got to stop that TV-radio thing. Listen!" He snatched the telegram back from her and read out what he had written. " 'Will sue Foundation, radio, and TV com-panies for millions if that program is broadcast without my permission.' "

Listening Marie thought, *They'll think—Mac will think—I'm a hysteric.*

She recalled that one of Carl's aphorisms described the reaction of high-level men to a hysterical woman. "The decision is made either to slap her down or cater to her."

She said shakily, "This is necessary, Walter? This is absolutely necessary?"

He answered in a hoarse *sotto voce*. "It absolutely mustn't be delayed another second."

"You're not giving me bad advice out of fear?"

"Marie, we mustn't let Carl get on the air till we know what he says."

There was truth in that. She nodded. "All right—send it!"

The stewardess took the telegram and presently came back with a second one. This one was from the attorney.

> Have begun negotiations with the Foundation. Legal situation obscure due to unique circumstances. See me when you get back. Many urgent factors to be discussed.

It was signed, "Bob L."

An hour before the plane landed, a third telegram was handed Marie. It was from Dr. MacKerrie:

> Okay, okay. Will meet your plane. Love, Mac.

Marie read the message, thinking, *They've decided to cater to me.*

She felt horribly ashamed.

"Mac" was waiting for them at the foot of the landing steps, a medium-built, smooth-faced, good-looking man in his early forties, very much the gentle, sensitive person she remembered.

It seemed that reporters were waiting inside, and he had conspired with the airline to ward them off her. He led Walter and her to a sedan that Marie recognized as belonging to the Hazzard Laboratories. The driver was a technician-employee who greeted her with an expression of regret and sympathy.

Mac's plan, it developed, was for her to go home and then later that day come down to the Brain Study Foundation for a screening of the first interview with Carl's brain, after which she could talk directly with Carl.

It was all so thoughtful and considerate, so lacking in any kind of threat, that Marie was taken aback when Walter leaned past her and said harshly, "As soon as I've taken Dr. Marie home, I'll come down and set up the conditions under which all this will be done. All right?"

If MacKerrie was startled by the words, he did not show it. "Whatever Dr. Marie and you agree on," he said quietly.

It was after three when Marie drove up to the Foundation door.

Walter was waiting and parked her car for her. When he came back, he reported in a low voice, "I've been here since noon, and the way it's arranged we'll have the screening first, then we'll go into the computer room, and you'll talk to Carl—"

"Have you seen the film yet?"

He shook his head. Silently, he led the way to the projection room.

Marie sat down in the semidarkness, a little blank, tense, not knowing what to expect.

When the screen lighted, it showed a plastic, transparent dome about five feet in diameter. The structure glittered with innumerable light reflections, and so several seconds went by before Marie was able to make out that inside was a curved, mirrorlike shape containing some clear liquid. Partly submerged in the liquid, a pink and gray object was visible. Different colored tubes were attached to this object from below, but they were harder to identify.

Marie gazed at the entire unusual conglomeration, not realizing. And then—

She gasped, closed her eyes and sank back into her seat, feeling faint.

Carl's brain!

A voice began to speak. Marie opened her eyes and saw that the picture of the brain had been replaced by the familiar figure of Dr. Angus MacKerrie. He was standing beside a machine that her experienced eyes recognized instantly as a computer.

MacKerrie said now, "The conversation you are about to hear will surprise you with its rapidity. Such speed is made possible by the fact that electronic devices can detect differences of a hundred millionth in the graph recording of a brain wave and because analogs of Dr. Hazzard's voice were made long ago for use with this computer machine."

He leaned over and pressed a button on the instrument. "Dr. Carl, this is Dr. MacKerrie. Are you receiving this message?"

He released the button.

The answer was in Carl's own voice. It was such a matter-of-fact answer, so natural, that Marie sat up in instant amazement. The voice said, "Yes, your question is, am I getting your inquiry?"

"Correct. Do you understand your situation, Doctor?"

"I understand it only too well. My brain has been removed from a now-dead body and is being kept alive in a nutrient solution."

"How do you feel about it?"

"I seem to be cheerful enough. Evidently, there is no feedback of anxiety from the mechanical equipment that is taking care of me—"

"Can you describe your exact sensory awareness?"

"It's like being in a pitch-black room, but I remember what the room is like. This seems to satisfy me for the time being."

"Aside from having no body, do you feel yourself to be normal?"

"That's difficult to answer. *My* feeling is, yes, I feel normal, but we both understand how subtly brain mechanisms can get out of order. Man receives his information from the outside world through his senses. I now have only brain impulses being triggered through a machine, and I have a storehouse of past data. We'll just have to wait and see what happens. Where's my wife?"

Marie started at the sudden change of direction of the conversation.

Dr. MacKerrie answered quietly, "She's on her way home from New Hampshire. Should be here in a few hours."

"Dear Marie. We had such a perfect marriage."

Marie's breath hissed abruptly in and out as she heard again a remark that Carl had made many times in the past. She recalled an aphorism of his: "A perfect marriage exists when a wife is bound to her husband by emotional ties that she does not even try to understand."

Carl had always insisted that their marriage lacked only the sexual component, and that—he had explained—"is due to my early ignorance of the nature of woman. Under correct circumstances, a wife will accept other feminine companionship in her husband's life." His belief was that he had been slow in realizing what those "correct circumstances" were, but he had several times challenged her: "If you can explain why you've stayed with me all these years, I'll reform instantly and become the husband image that you think you want."

Marie had always disdained to reply. The early disaster to her marriage had numbed her, turned her thought and feeling toward the pure realm of science. And because there had never been another man, divorce had seemed pointless.

In the seat beside her, Walter suddenly grew rigid. His fingers convulsively grabbed her arm.

As she turned her attention again to the screen, she realized Dr. MacKerrie had asked a very important question:

". . . Doctor, the person who ran you down has not yet been apprehended. Can you give the police a clue?"

Marie held her breath as Carl said, "It was a very confused moment for me. I have some impressions, but I need time to sort them out. Until I do will you see that I am protected from further harm?"

"The police have stationed a guard, so have no fear."

Marie sighed and breathed again. Walter let go of her arm—as Dr. MacKerrie continued: "What do you think should be your future activity, Dr. Carl?"

"Scientific, of course. My reasoning powers seem unaffected by what has happened."

The interview ended with Dr. MacKerrie saying, "Dr. Carl, thank you. Do you have any parting words for the audience out there?"

"Yes, I hope to speak to you all again soon."

"That shall most certainly happen," said MacKerrie in a hearty voice.

CHAPTER III

The screen went blank.

The lights came on.

Walter stood up with a quick, nervous movement, his lean face twisted. "That whole section about who ran him down has to come out," he said sharply.

Marie stared at him in amazement. But as she saw his face, so intent, so self-absorbed, so serious, she thought anxiously, "Is it possible I'm not facing up to the danger in this?"

For minutes now she had even been feeling an intense excitement at the marvelous scientific achievement they had witnessed. She hesitated, then said, "Be sure, also, to have them eliminate the reference to my being on the way home. That dates it, which it shouldn't do."

Walter hurried into the projection room. When he emerged, he said almost cheerfully, "Well, that's settled. I'll check again later to make sure. But right now—" An expression of concern creased his face. "Marie, you're going to have to brace yourself."

"For what?" Surprised.

"Where we're going now, Carl's brain is visible."

Marie shrank, remembering her reaction to the film image.

Walter continued. "MacKerrie figured you'd better get used to it from the start."

He now led her to a room that had a typical TV camera standing in the center of the floor and, at one end, the computer that she had seen in the film.

Walter motioned her toward it. "There's a blue button," he said.

As Marie walked forward, she glimpsed something beyond the machine: the glass dome, with Carl's brain inside. She looked away hastily and, having located the button, stood with her back to the dome and stared straight at the camera that Walter now focused on her.

Walter explained matter-of-factly, "I agreed to the filming of this interview because it would have looked suspicious if I had refused."

Marie, who was convinced that the whole affair looked highly suspicious already, was unhappily silent.

Walter went on. "Of course, I made the agreement contingent on my operating the camera and on you and me being alone with Carl during the interview. They acceded. You'll notice they pulled the police guard out into the corridor."

Marie hadn't noticed. She couldn't recall making any observation at all in the hallway.

"Ready?" Walter asked.

Marie hesitated. She wanted to point out to him the danger of secrecy. People would wonder.

Walter continued. "Remember, the computer has analogs only for your voice and of course for Carl's. So Carl will get the message when you speak, but what I say will not reach him. And he gets *your* message when your finger presses that button, not before you press it or after you let go. If you bear these simple truths in mind, we can say or do anything, and he'll never know unless we tell him. Now, is there anything that's not clear?"

Marie said simply, "What are we here for?"

His lean body hunched a little. His voice was suddenly jerky. "What's on his mind about that accusation he made. Get him to your lab where you and I can have control of all his communication."

Marie swallowed, nodded. If that were achieved, this nightmare of pressure might end as abruptly as it had begun.

She waited hopefully for the signal.

When the little red dot below the camera lens blinked on, she pressed the blue button firmly with her finger, held it down, and said, "Carl, it's Marie."

The reply came with the same speed that had already startled her in the film. "Marie, I'm so glad you're here. I need most desperately to talk to you."

"Are you all right, my dear?"

The affectionate term cost her no effort. Carl had always insisted that she call him dear or darling "for the sake of the amenities, my sweet." It meant nothing then— or now.

"My darling," said Carl, "a terrible thing has happened to me. I have become a nothing, a mind suspended in a great night. You must never leave me. I need you more than ever."

Marie held herself detached from the emotion in his appeal. She said in an even voice, "Perhaps, I should take you home."

"As soon as possible," was the reply. "I've got to be there with you."

"I'll speak to Dr. MacKerrie," Marie said. "I'm sure it can be arranged—if you wish it."

"I can't tell you how strongly I wish it." He must have

realized she was willing, for he said, "I seem to have slept a lot since the operation, but in between I'm in this total blackness."

Marie hardened her heart. "Is there anything I can do for you right now, darling?" she asked.

Pause.

"Marie, is this being broadcast?"

She was instantly tense. "It's being tape recorded for later broadcast."

"I want to say something to you personally."

"Go ahead."

"Can you turn the camera off and send the cameraman away?"

She glanced at Walter, who nodded. The little red dot in the camera went black.

"The camera is off, Carl, and the cameraman has gone off to have a smoke."

"Marie, is everything all right?"

"As well as can be."

"You haven't got yourself into some impossible situation?"

Marie smiled a suddenly strained smile. She recognized that behind the question was an old attitude of Carl's that had always irritated her: his conviction that, left to herself, she would quickly get into trouble.

"No, I am not in some impossible situation." She spoke with asperity.

"Don't be angry, darling. But when I think of you out there without me, it bothers me."

It struck Marie that Carl still had all his old capacity to enrage her. She was about to make another hot reply when she grew aware that Walter was waving at her frantically. Carefully, feeling flushed, she took her finger off the button and looked at him questioningly.

Walter said, "Ask him what kind of impossible situation?"

It cost Marie an effort to remember what she and Walter were trying to do. She asked the question.

Carl replied, "Marie, this situation has a lot more energy in it than you seem to realize. I feel as if I have to save you from being forced into some fantastic involvement—the kind that a woman's emotions get her into. You know my theories—"

She knew them well and hated them.

Walter was waving. "Ask him what he means by energy."

Since it was an old term of Carl's, Marie was able to explain.

Carl's view of human behavior was that it was wholly mechanical. People did what they were impelled to by the physics and chemistry of their internal structure and by the electromagnetic flows in the body and brain. This, he believed, was true even in normal circumstances, though not so apparent.

It was visibly true when a threat stimulated the emotion of fear.

When the factors of threat and fear increased in intensity, the energy flows involved were so strong that they dominated the person.

Progressively, this energy overwhelmed normal restraint, morality, all human qualities. The situation thereupon found its exact solution, to which all parties connected with it conformed like so many puppets.

Marie finished impatiently. "Carl was always expounding on the low-levelness of human beings while behaving like a low-level human being himself."

Walter said in a tense voice, "Ask him what energy he thinks is in this situation."

The request again brought Marie out of her critical, subjective feelings. In a subdued voice, she passed on the request.

Carl replied, "My dear, consider! Somebody ran me down. Have they captured him? I hate to tell you this, but my first feeling was that it was Walter. Naturally, I realize how such a possibility might affect you in view of what's been going on between you two. Now, Marie, if he is guilty, suppose the police trace him. Marie, I urge you—be careful! The energy is almost boundless in human terms."

He broke off. "Have you talked with Walter?"

His words were now so highly charged that Marie looked helplessly at Walter. From behind the camera Walter said quietly, "Tell him yes. We've got to know, Marie. Tell him I told you about his firing me and why."

Swiftly, she pressed the button and made the communication.

Carl replied, "Ask Walter to remain on the job. And,

Marie, if you are involved with him, withdraw. You know what I believe in connection with murder. It's the greatest energy of all, exerts the greatest pressure."

Marie had hold of herself. She said steadily, "Carl, remember your past jealousies—how you would see things that weren't there. I'm sure somewhere in your mind you know very well that this is just one more piece of nonsense like that. Your feeling, as you call it, that Walter ran you down is in this category, isn't it? So now, listen! I'm not involved with him. Moreover, I shall not get involved. You destroyed me as a woman, and if you want my good will in this situation—which you can have—you'll stop those kinds of thoughts and settle down to the kind of scientific reasoning and scientific work that should engage your attention from now on."

After she had spoken the words, every one true, she shook her head wonderingly at Walter.

He motioned her again to release the button. When she had done so, he said urgently, "Marie, he must have some scheme here."

Marie couldn't imagine what it might be.

Walter continued. "I want you to think, is there anything he's ever done that would give us a clue to his purposes? Those jealous rages of his—what else was there to the pattern? From the way you've described them, he must have been mentally deranged each time."

Marie shook her head numbly.

The pattern had always been jealousy for no reason, followed by extreme remorse.

On every occasion she had been totally innocent of involvement with a man.

She said slowly, "Carl always said that every human being had his own way of having a nervous breakdown. But except for the periods of crazy jealousy, I never saw him in any state except a kind of ice-cold, good-humored cynicism."

"Marie—" It was Carl— "I want you to promise to let me remain with you. If you do, I'll do exactly as you want. I don't wish to be with all these strangers. You'll bear that in mind, won't you, sweetheart?"

"Of course, you stay with me, my dear," said Marie, relieved.

As Walter and she left the building a little later, Walter

said, "What was that business about murder being the biggest energy?"

Marie explained. Murder and murderers had always fascinated Carl. Murder had to be secret, he believed.

"A murderer, my dear," Carl had said more than once, "is in sufficient danger if he alone knows that he did it. Even then the pressure on him is colossal. However, if the secret is in the head of one other person, he is doomed or he has to kill that person."

Walter seemed to consider that, for he was silent. He said finally, "I've been ransacking my brains, trying to think how I can prove that there was no involvement between us. For example, I've been impotent ever since, in my late twenties, I discovered that my wife was sleeping with every male member of the faculty at the college where I taught."

Marie thought at that point: "What a fantastic admission he's making." But it explained a lot about him.

Walter was continuing earnestly. "But how can I ever establish such a subjective condition?" He shook his head. "No, Marie, I'm afraid we're at the beginning, not the end of this business."

Marie's thought had leaped to something else: Walter's behavior. She taxed him with it. "Walter, I have to speak to you about how suspicious your actions must have seemed to MacKerrie and the others."

Walter shook his head, and suddenly the dark, serious look was gone. He smiled faintly. "Don't worry," he said confidently, "they'll think you're behind it, and everybody knows that women are like that."

"Like what?"

"Unreasonable, irrational."

"I am *not* irrational," said Marie.

"I know, but they don't know," said Walter. "No harm in taking advantage of the general reputation."

"But you're ruining me," she cried.

He patted her arm. "Now, look, Marie, no woman can escape the opinion of men on this subject. Notice, there's not an argument from anyone."

He added, "Do you mind if I give you some advice?"

Marie hesitated. She was remembering an aphorism of Carl's: "The attempt to control the widow begins not later than the funeral: usually, it is well started while her lord and master is still gasping for a few last breaths."

She had to admit, after a moment, that this was different. What control Walter was exercising had been made necessary by the madness of the author of the aphorism.

She was about to agree that she would hear his advice when Walter, not waiting, said, "No one objects to a new widow staying in seclusion for a few days. Take full advantage of that."

The meaning of the word, spoken aloud, startled Marie. "But I'm not a widow," she protested.

Walter blinked at her, his handsome, boyish face intent again, "If you're not a widow, what are you?" he asked, astonished.

Marie had no answer for that, but she said presently, "I'll stay out of sight if that's what you want—except for my attorney."

"Good," said Walter.

CHAPTER IV

Her appointment was for two.

On the dot, a young man walked into the office where Marie waited. He radiated high spirits, and he introduced himself as Robert Lindley, the son of the senior partner.

Marie had never met him, but she recalled that Carl had taken a fancy to him. "My type!" Carl had said laconically. It was not a recommendation to her, but after her first quick look at this young man's glowing face she decided to reserve judgment.

The youthful attorney held in his hand a document that Marie presumed was the will. He stood there in his immaculate, neatly pressed suit behind a gleaming desk. Beyond was a glistening, clean window overlooking the boulevard . . . Stood there and gazed at Marie with his head held slightly slantwise and his eyes half closed, speculatively.

"Your husband was very foolish," he said. "You're better looking than they are."

Marie surmised that "they" were Carl's mistresses. She was taken aback by the plural term. She had always assumed that Carl had one girl friend at a time, none for very long, and a large accumulation of discards over a decade and a half of philandering.

The young man went on. "In asking to have the will read to you privately, I presume you are taking the attitude that your husband is legally dead."

Marie said, "I expect simply to comply with the law."

"There is no law." His eyes were eager. "I'd like to establish a precedent. Dr. MacKerrie tells me that only the brain thinks; it has been established that no other part of the body plays an important role in behavior and none at all in the thinking process."

Marie realized that almost without preliminary they were into the heart of her visit.

Lindley sat down and tapped the will with one finger. "This," he said, "leaves the bulk of the estate to you but provides allowances for three women in the event of his death."

"Three!" said Marie involuntarily.

She closed her eyes and shrank inwardly as she thought of the worldwide publicity that such a trio of bequests would receive.

When she opened her eyes again, young Lindley was gazing at her soberly but with shining gaze. He said softly, "They're identified as former secretaries on special projects, but still—why don't we go in and ask the court to declare your husband legally alive?"

"But—"

She stopped. And then, as she sat there in a partial haze, she heard his voice coolly explaining that the other beneficiaries named in the will could scarcely expect to collect until the person who had made the will was legally declared dead.

"It's your choice, Dr. Marie," said the attorney.

Marie stirred to the realization that the young man was coming around his desk. He bent over her anxiously. "I thought you knew," he said. "Your husband assured me that he had kept nothing from you. Naturally, I personally was amazed at his revelation."

Marie shook her head. "It's not that."

Exactly what held her from instant agreement, Marie could not decide. Vague thoughts and feelings, an overall reluctance to be tied down; she could formulate nothing clearly.

Aloud, she said, "Those bequests! Am I the administrator? Would I be the one who signed the checks?"

"The bequests have an initial claim on the estate. But this office could make the payments. The amount is six hundred dollars each—a total of eighteen hundred a month."

"And it comes first?"

"I'm afraid so."

Marie did a mental calculation. Twenty-one thousand six hundred a year.

Eeee! she thought.

She settled herself in her chair, feeling slim and prim and very determined.

"Let's fight to have him declared alive!" she said.

"Good girl!" He was glowing. "This will be a precedent."

His clean-cut face grew serious again. "Now you realize that we'll have a better chance to get such a court order if there's no contest."

Marie was instantly wary. "What does that mean?"

He spread his hands. "Let me approach these women. Make them an offer of, say, two hundred dollars a month for three years, quietly, without any publicity. I think they'll take it rather than risk losing everything."

Marie remembered her initial reservations about this young man. He was getting from her one agreement at a time, a salesman's trick. She pointed this out, accusingly, then finished. "If I agree to this, what else have you got up your sleeve?"

Young Lindley smiled. He suddenly looked very boyish. "Two more things," he said. "One is business and has to do with the Non-Pareil Corporation and its affairs. That was always handled by Coster, Pierce and Drew, who specialize in corporation law."

Marie said scathingly, "You can be sure Carl didn't dare bring up to *them* the idea of hiring a detective to follow his wife. But—" she nodded— "I agree. Non-Pareil is legally a different situation."

"Still," persisted Lindley, "that stock is disposed of in this will. It's left to you. We'll have to have the court give you the voting power involved."

Marie said she understood, and added, "And what's the

second other thing on your mind? I gather it's not business."

"No, it's personal," Lindley admitted. "But aside from a personal embarrassment you won't basically mind it."

Marie wanted to know what it was.

"Now, look," he pleaded, "I'm too young to talk to you like a Dutch uncle, right?"

"Well—"

"You'll have to picture me as a graybeard in a doctor's office, looking owlishly at you over my glasses. Can you do that?"

Marie laughed at the ridiculous portrait he had conjured with his words. But she merely stared at him expectantly. And unsuspecting.

The young man pulled a clean, white handkerchief from a pocket of his dark gray suit and wiped his suddenly perspiring face with it. "I'm not good at old age and much too smart for the age I am," he muttered, "so I'll just say it: Your husband has only been dead a few days—I use the word dead in the sense of incapacitated. If you were to have a baby in nine months and ten days plus a week or so, it would still be considered his—if you said it was, and if you had done nothing in the meanwhile to arouse any suspicions."

Time stopped.

Slowly, the room settled back to a semblance of normalcy, though she continued to be caught in what seemed to be a tunnel-vision phenomenon, with walls of blackness on either side.

"What on earth are you talking about?" she breathed.

The figure at the far end of the tunnel said in a hollow voice, "Walter!"

This time she didn't sink. She sat there, feeling empty except for the ice-cold lump of fear in her stomach.

She heard the man's voice say that two weeks ago Carl had come to this very office and had instructed young Lindley to hire a detective to spy on Marie and Walter.

"It never happened," the lawyer said. "We wrote up the new will, but he didn't come in to sign it, and he canceled the detective before he ever started, and sent you to visit your parents. The rest you know."

Marie was recovering. She said grimly, "Are you quite finished?"

He looked at her, a strange expression in his gray eyes. "Evidently," he said soberly.

"Good. Now let's get back to reality."

"It was a hard thing to say to a woman," he defended, "but if there was any truth in your husband's belief, it provided a solution which would satisfy all the basic human needs and motives. You do want a child, don't you?"

He added hastily, "Remember, if he's declared alive, it'll be awfully difficult to divorce a man in his condition. So it's now or never."

Marie said, "Why not ask your father to tell you how many times this pattern has occurred before? The threat of changing the will, hiring the detective, calling off the detective before he can discover there's nothing to it— I've really had quite a trying marital situation, Mr. Lindley."

The attorney was silent; finally he said, "I don't think I should say anymore except—what are your instructions?"

"You don't believe me?" Marie said hopelessly.

"Of course I do," he answered in a hearty voice. Too hearty.

"I suppose," said Marie, "it is hard to believe that a woman should remain unattached for fourteen years."

Young Lindley was discreetly silent.

Marie stood up. "When can we go to court?" she asked in a flat voice.

Lindley responded eagerly. "The sooner the better. I'll get on it today."

As Marie left the law office and went down to the parking lot in the bright afternoon sunshine, she had a feeling of defeat. She thought, *I can't really escape what Carl has done. Everywhere I turn, the lie has preceded me.*

Well, she conceded, almost everywhere.

CHAPTER V

As she came up to her house, Marie saw that a large van was turning slowly into the driveway of the laboratory. She drew up behind it, parked her car, and then watched as it edged up—as slowly—toward the unloading platform of the laboratory. The great doors swung open.

Dr. MacKerrie stepped onto the loading platform; and, as Marie came up, and Walter and several members of the lab staff came out and watched, the surgeon supervised the unloading of Carl's brain and of the accompanying equipment. A space had been made in a special room where temperature controls could be maintained. It was there that Carl's future home was established.

MacKerrie moved into one of the cottages.

Walter came up to the house to find out what the attorney had said.

Marie had made her peace with Lindley's crazy ideas while driving home. And so she was amazed when she explained what had happened to see the color drain from Walter's face. His body grew so tense that she stared at him, alarmed.

Abruptly, red stained his cheeks. He said in a low, vicious tone, "Tell that G— D— fool to mind his G— D— business."

He stepped forward and gripped her shoulders with a stonelike grip. He said in a voice that was as taut as drawn wire, "What did you admit to him?"

"Nothing!" She whispered her answer.

She was too astounded, in too much agony, completely overwhelmed, and made completely guilty by his awful anger. She saw what he was thinking: that young Lindley had trapped a confession from her. His reaction focused in her mind the deadly picture: that *any* suspicion against him could set in motion forces that could ruin him.

Abruptly, the pain became unbearable. She began to struggle. "Let me go!" she gasped. "You're hurting me."

As quickly as it had started, his violence ended.

He released her. Then caught her as she reeled in a partial faint. He said in a half-groan, "Marie, forgive me!"

Marie stood shakily, rubbing her shoulders. But she had gone through all of his emotions and thoughts in a *rapport of logic*—as Carl had once described the phenomenon of simultaneous comprehension; and so she said in a low voice, "There's nothing to forgive. I understand—"

She stopped. Because understanding made no difference. Her body was trembling from head to foot. "Help me!" she whispered.

She allowed Walter to assist her to a couch. She lay there and trembled.

And trembled.

She mumbled, "Call Dr. MacKerrie. I need a sedative."

Walter hesitated; and she felt an instant anger at him, for he was clearly having some cautious thought that downrated her condition as being of secondary importance.

Walter crouched a little and said slowly, "Some other doctor, not Mac."

"For God's sake," she said, "this is an emergency."

Walter started for the door, pushed by her urgency. Then he stopped, turned. "No," he said, and there was complete determination in his voice. "Not Mac. I refuse to involve him in any way."

Marie scrambled to her feet and ran for the door. She flung it open. "Mrs. Gray!" she yelled.

The housekeeper came hurrying from the kitchen. "I'm not well," Marie sobbed. "Get Dr. MacKerrie. In Cottage D."

Walter pushed past her. "I'll get him," he said in a low voice.

Marie caught a glimpse of his white face as he went down the hall and out of the house.

MacKerrie gave her a tranquilizer. At least that was what he called it. He was cool, professional, competent. She began to feel better, and she said to him apologetically, "I think this business suddenly hit me."

It was the explanation she had made up hastily while she lay there waiting, hating herself for being so overwrought.

Dr. MacKerrie nodded, patted her hand, and went out with, "Call me if you need me."

When they were alone again, Walter sat, leaning forward, one hand shading his eyes. He looked utterly dejected.

Marie sat up and said, "I'm sorry."

Walter straightened slowly. "This is not personal," he said. "I hope you'll believe that. But the thought is in my mind, and I might as well say it. This is all we need: a hysterical woman."

Marie had no answer. Never in her whole life had she been so completely unstrung.

Walter said, "For the first time what you said that first day makes meaning to me—about where a murder is known to two people, the murderer is doomed. Now, I'm not a murderer, but I could be made out to be one. And I'm scared. In all my pictures of this situation, I never once visualized you falling apart."

Marie whispered, "It was the awful shock of your anger and the terrible pain of the way you grabbed me. I can't imagine it ever happening again. I really can't."

She added, "And I don't think I made any admissions to Mr. Lindley."

As she reported her exact conversation with the young attorney, Walter brightened. His face grew dark as she came again to the part where Lindley had suggested that they have a child, but he relaxed gradually as she reported her reaction.

She was thinking again. She said earnestly, "I really don't think he was scheming against me. After all, I'm a client from whom he will receive not less than five thousand a year, sometimes as much as ten."

"That much?" Walter sounded surprised.

"We have to have all those detailed contracts," she said. "Carl proved to me long ago that we can't afford a single mix-up or omission."

"I see." Walter seemed more at ease. He hesitated; then he said, "This is not for now, what I'm going to say, and I'm awfully reluctant to make any suggestions on business. But I have a brother who is an attorney, and my feeling is that a little later, after Lindley has fixed it with these women and got Carl declared legally alive, that you switch your legal affairs over to him. Will you consider that? I *know* he'll protect us."

"Of course I'll consider it," said guilty Marie, anxious to make amends.

When Walter had gone, Marie sagged back on the settee, and she had the infinitely sad realization that she could never trust herself again.

As she lay there, she gradually became aware that the trembling feeling was still there, deep inside her.

Waiting.

The following morning there was a long distance call from an Eastern university. A large amount of Hazzard equipment was wanted for a new NASA project. Somebody, however, would have to go there and personally obtain the specifications. In the past Carl had made such journeys.

After discussion it was clear that either Marie and one of

the other physicists would have to go together, or Walter by himself. No one else was qualified.

Marie tried to assign the task to Walter, but he didn't want to go.

"I shouldn't leave this situation," he told her nervously. "Who knows what will happen when I'm away? It's too soon for me to take trips anywhere."

Marie was impatient. "You're going to have to do this work if you remain chief physicist. And besides, what will you do here that I can't?"

He gazed at her gloomily. "I can't trust anyone to protect me the way I can protect myself, least of all a woman. That's practically an axiom."

"Now, look, you want the job as chief physicist, don't you?"

"I guess so." His attention seemed to be far away.

"Then we've got to act as if everything is normal. Since I can talk to Carl, I should be here. You don't want to leave him here to Mac?"

Late in the afternoon, she drove a reluctant Walter to the airport. He was so jittery that he failed to say good-by to her; he simply walked through the gate and never looked back.

As she drove home, Marie realized it was a relief to be away from the tense atmosphere of terror that had literally radiated from Walter.

CHAPTER VI

Home. Continued cheerfulness. Twice, she found herself humming gaily under her breath. She ate dinner alone but happily and afterward started a novel—it was a long time since she had found pleasure in reading for fun.

A few minutes after nine her phone rang. It was Dr. MacKerrie. "I wonder if I could come over and talk to you?" he said.

"Would tomorrow do as well?" she asked. "I was about to go to bed."

Surprisingly, he insisted.

He came in, a gravely smiling, medium tall, good-looking man in his forties, somehow seeming a little too gentle, lacking both Carl's and Walter's sternness. Marie invited him to sit in a chair facing her. He drew it up close to hers and began in a low voice:

"Marie, as you know, and as I told the police inspector the other day, you and I are the only people who have carried on conversations with Carl."

A distinct shock, palpable, unpleasant, went through Marie at the reference to a police officer. It cost her an effort, but presently she was able to say, "Yes?"

His gray-blue eyes gazed quietly into hers. "So essentially whatever Carl had said, you and I are the only ones to whom he has said it."

Crash!

It took Marie a moment to come out of a peculiar confusion that had suddenly gripped her to realize that she had dropped her ashtray.

She grew aware of MacKerrie, smiling faintly, down on his knees, scraping up the debris. "Still nervous, I see," he said lightly.

Marie knelt beside him and tried awkwardly to help him with the ashes. What she had in mind was not clear, for inside she was shattering more every instant. She had a vague impulse to enlist his good will, a strong desire to stop him from saying anything more than he already had.

She believed that he knew. That Carl had told him.

She started to mumble something about Carl's side of the story not being reliable—when it happened.

She was being held. Mac's face came toward hers, and his lips pressed her cheeks and then her lips. "Don't worry!" he whispered. "I'm on your side. I hope you'll be on mine."

During the rapid minutes that followed she only dimly realized what his price was, but she was numbly aware that she was paying it.

That was the overall feeling: a numbness from head to foot.

After Mac had gone, Marie gradually came to life. Her body emerged from its partial paralysis. She remembered the warmth of his words and the intense emotion that had radiated from him.

No threat at all, only love.

Was it possible that the fear he had stimulated in her had projected from a madness in her brain?

Whatever the cause, she had betrayed her own truth, her lifetime code, the entire meaningfulness of her resistance to Carl's infidelity—

Lying there in the darkness, remembering, she thought, appalled, "I never did a thing like that before."

It had been sex in color experienced by a woman who had previously operated only in black and white.

She had offered herself at some primitive level of being. She had begged him in her manner and behavior to take her and, by doing so, to take care of her and protect her. And through all the numbness, she had paid the price of her begging by responding to him with passion and uncontrollable excitement.

Carl, when they were first married, had never evoked from her such a total intensity of feeling.

Guilt and shame flooded up into her consciousness like stained water pouring from a broken main.

The memory was finally blotted out by the darkness of sleep.

When she woke in the morning, she felt rational once more, and she had the kind of solution that she recognized came from guilty repentance.

It was over.

It must remain a secret, buried deep in her shamed conscience.

It must not happen again.

Exactly what she would say to Dr. MacKerrie was not clear. But something that cut him off without turning him against her.

But she had an uneasy memory.

Carl had said more than once, "My dear, you play with total skill the lowest female game of all, the game of needing to be taken care of. With me, you've got yourself into such an impregnable moral position that I'm taking care of you without any recompense. But one of these days you may discover how much you are actually willing to do to satisfy that need."

It seemed to Marie that after last night she had no defense against the analysis. She had been woman incarnate at an unsuspected, desperate level.

She dressed, dreading the meeting with Mac but bracing for it, accepting that it must take place.

Yet in the end, it was her unwillingness that won; and she remained indoors, her door locked, her blinds drawn. The phone rang, but she did not answer. She had instructed Mrs. Gray to say that she was not in to anyone.

As she lay in the semidarkness, Marie kept her mind mostly blank. She no longer questioned the impulse to remain withdrawn and hidden. The intuition that had guided her to it had been shaped by all the reluctant muscles and cells in her body: the reluctance to confront someone suddenly with a shocking statement of reversal.

Now it would gradually sink into Mac that something was wrong. And so when she finally told him, he would be resigned to the rejection.

She remained secluded all the next day. But when a wire from Walter at seven established that he would be flying back by the following evening, it occurred to her that she ought to have her problem with MacKerrie out of the way before Walter came back on the scene.

She waited for nightfall and then went for a walk in the garden. A minute later, footsteps sounded, and MacKerrie fell into step beside her.

"Marie, what's wrong?"

His shadowed body hovered in the darkness of the summer night in an attitude of concern; his voice was anxious.

"The wrongness is entirely in you," she said. "I was in a very disturbed state, and you had no right to take advantage of that; you of all people, a doctor."

They had stopped. But she realized from the way he stood that he was not feeling regret or guilt. "Marie," he said in a low voice, "I'm not your doctor. And when a woman responds to a man the way you responded to me, she can't just slough him off."

Marie said steadily, "I respect you, but I don't love you. I am not in the market for a lover or a husband."

He seemed to be thinking. Then he said, "Can I come in some time and tell you the story of my life and my first marriage?"

111

The question made her aware of how little she knew about this man. "Tell me now!" she said.

Mac's marital story was brief. His wife was in a mental institution, hopelessly insane. Because of her condition he had become interested in the human brain as a physiological phenomenon.

"After all," he said, "I'm a surgeon and not a psychiatrist. Whatever the self may be, it thinks and operates through an organic mechanism that can be dissected. In human beings that mechanism—the brain—is sufficiently complex to engage my attention as an object of research from now on."

Marie made no comment. MacKerrie's skill in his specialty was a byword, almost—since his removal of Carl's brain—the last word.

It seemed to her that his disinterest in the psychological aspects of his wife's mental condition proved something. Guilt, perhaps. But also unawareness.

She analyzed that, aside from his personal warmth—which was always there—Dr. MacKerrie didn't want to know what people felt or why they felt it.

But his story gave her more ammunition.

She said, puzzled, "As I understand it—and this is not personal, has nothing to do with me—you're expecting some good woman to tolerate this situation you're in, comfort you, and live in some permanent, damaged existence in relation to you? Is that right?"

If she had hoped to disturb him, she was mistaken. He said simply, "I was hoping that you would love me and, yes, tolerate my condition."

Marie said with determination, "Under the circumstances of your position here, I think that I have the right to ask you to promise that you will never again bring up any personal thing with me. Will you promise?"

"No."

The instant refusal reminded Marie of another observation of that redoubtable scientist-philosopher, Dr. Carl Hazzard: "If somebody turns you down, honey, it's because he feels himself to be one-up. If he's wrong about that, give him a shove; he'll fall over. But if he's right, don't say anymore. Words have no meaning against a position of power."

Marie wondered, *In what way does Mac feel one-up?*

She tested him. "Why won't you promise? Give me one good reason."

MacKerrie said gently, "If you'll tell me what made you surrender to me the other night, I'll answer that."

It was, of course, impossible for her to say that she feared that he would believe Carl's lie and that she had, in her total anxiety, dissolved into a jellylike substance that begged for mercy.

So she repeated, "I've already told you. You took advantage of a woman in a partial state of nervous breakdown."

Silence.

She urged, "What have you to say to that?"

"Marie—" MacKerrie's voice was patient— "Every man has run into the problem that a woman has in our society. When she gives in to a normal impulse, she immediately feels vulnerable and must justify it on some extreme level. I understand the physiology of your response to me, and that's all I ever need. I leave your present impulse to justify to those elements in society that, as a scientist, I long ago learned to ignore. The fact that you responded to me physically in the remarkable way that you did shows that we are well mated. All the rest is some kind of feminine smoke screen, the kind of thing, as I said before, that women do. Have I answered you?"

She turned abruptly and left him.

At least, she had told him.

The rest depended on how much he really knew.

She slept with the aid of a sleeping pill, but it was a disturbed, dream-filled sleep.

And she remembered none of the dreams.

CHAPTER VII

Walter flew in the next night. He brought with him a stack of orders. Particularly wanted was a whole group of custom items for low temperature work with helium. Some of the equipment would sell for as much as $50,000 each, and the whole totaled more than a million dollars.

The great success of his journey seemed to have lifted his spirits. "It was actually good to get away," he said.

Shortly after he had gone off to unpack, the phone rang. Marie answered and felt a shock as she heard Mac's voice, tense and disturbed, at the other end.

"Marie, I'm very ill. Could you call a doctor?"

She had an instant series of thoughts that had never occurred to her before. *He believes Walter and I are having an affair. He knows Walter is now back, and he's gone into a thing on it. Well, it's his breakdown, his foolishness, not mine.*

What startled her was the sudden realization that Mac must have made love to her thinking that he was encroaching on Walter's domain.

Abruptly, she felt extremely critical of him and said sharply, "If you can phone me, surely you can call your own doctor."

Mac answered in a griefy voice. "I'll be here all night, ill. Think of me, will you?"

"Naturally," said Marie angrily and hung up.

It occurred to her that Mac might phone her throughout the night in the belief that Walter was with her. The possibility aroused all the frustration, helplessness, and resentment that she had felt over her situation.

. . . All these people who believed something about her that was not so, and there was nothing she could do or say that would change their minds.

She removed her phone receiver from its hook and laid it down out of sight on the floor.

The night passed without any further problem.

As she ate an early breakfast the next morning, she thought, *Actually, it's men who are doomed. They're hopelessly caught up in this sex thing. But aside from that, they are probably quite human.*

It seemed to her that she had made an important observation, and it was her own for a change, not Carl's.

It was an important day.

In court, shortly before noon, the disembodied brain of Dr. Carl Hazzard was declared "a living person."

Dr. Marie Hazzard was appointed the brain's official guardian, with the recommendation that she utilize every resource of modern science, particularly the skill and knowledge of the Brain Study Foundation, "to maintain the fragile thread of life remaining to your famous husband."

Having completed the basic statement, the judge, a large, comfortable-looking man, smiled down at her in a friendly fashion and said, "Dr. Marie, permit me to congratulate you on the occasion of this historic judgment. Your firm determination to grant to Dr. Carl the stature of a living being is in the highest tradition of the humanitarianism of today's scientific elite and is a personal triumph of ethics and morality for a woman."

On the way out of the courtroom attorney Lindley walked along the corridor with her and said in a low voice, "That was an unexpected eulogy from his honor. It will be quoted all over the world. A movie star could shuffle out from under that but not a Nobel Prize winner in physics."

Marie knew what he meant. No divorce. An exemplary public life. Complete conformance to the rules.

The young man continued. "It makes me regret all the more that there was no physical evidence that the wife of the famous scientist would bear his child, conceived a few days before his untimely accident. Any possibility that I can still make such an announcement to the press?"

Remembering Walter's reaction to her earlier discussion with this young man, Marie said unhappily, "You evidently have come to believe my husband's exotic fantasies. I'm sorry to report, in view of your concern, that what you suggested was never possible."

"Too bad." He shook his head regretfully. "Sorry I scared Walter off."

It was direct, showed such a fixed view, that Marie thought, shocked, *What is he up to?*

Before she could speak, young Lindley said, "Remember, whatever emotions others may have, attorney's files are the calm repositories of many a family skeleton. Since it is not my business to prove any man's guilt but merely to advise him or her what course to pursue, my knowledge is not dangerous to you or Walter. Not that I know anything more than your husband told me."

Marie said quickly, "I've told you Carl was an extremely jealous man. He went through cycles like this, as you would discover if you asked your father."

The young man nodded judicially. "A common characteristic of some males; probably goes back to the Neanderthal."

She braced herself, then said icily, "I can't understand why you would bring up such an idea a second time."

Bob Lindley said in an even tone, "An attorney tells his client what he considers necessary—or would you rather have some other legal firm represent you?"

So that was it?

Marie sighed. He was letting her know that his hold on her had the deadly hook of secret knowledge. If young Lindley had anything to do with it, his firm would represent her from now on.

He must have had an intuition. Perhaps he knew about Walter's lawyer brother. Hard to believe. Yet how else explain this almost open blackmail?

Marie repressed her anxiety. "Don't be silly," she said lightly. "I am completely satisfied with your legal work. Just don't bring up that foolishness again."

"If that's the way you want it," said Bob Lindley, "let's consider it all as if it were never said."

That would be a little difficult, Marie reflected grimly, as they presently separated. He had made his point with an intensity that revealed her tolerant morning philosophizing to be unrealistic.

Carl is right, she thought. *It's women who are doomed. All these men are getting what they want, while I—*

She couldn't quite decide about herself. She *felt* as if she were the victim of remorseless circumstance.

CHAPTER VIII

At the time of the award of the Nobel Prize, a famous artist had painted Carl and herself—separate portraits. As with so many moderns, he had proved himself incapable of getting a good likeness, but for Carl he had managed an idealized face with a touch of the diabolic in the eyes.

Carl had been delighted. He had always had the conviction that, except for his eyes, he really presented a prosaic appearance: gaunt body, sunken cheeks—but intense, burning eyes.

It was this portrait that Marie had mounted in the brain room.

For some days, construction had been proceeding around the brain. Carl had expressed a fear that something might fall on the dome that housed him. And so a curved, steel, protective structure had now been fitted on steel girders above him. It seemed to Marie that with such a barrier even a stray meteorite would have a hard time killing him.

A day went by. Then more days.

Marie began to breathe easier. She presumed that the entire turmoil that had followed Carl's accident was still continuing—the police, Mac, the other women—but at least they were all being quiet about it.

Let them continue that way!

Suddenly, one day at noon the door to her apartment opened, and Walter strode in. And what was surprising was that he had not given her the usual courtesy notice by phone that he was coming.

Nor had he knocked.

He was thin-lipped, taut. "I've just been talking to Mac," he said grimly.

She had parted her lips to speak sharply to him about the manner of his intrusion. Now she felt a pang. "Mac?" she echoed.

"He confided to me that he is in love with you and that he has a good reason to believe that you love him."

She backed away from the wild light in his eyes. "He has no reason," she said. "But why are you concerned?"

Walter stepped forward, and before she realized his intent, his hand came up. Deliberately, he slapped her face. He said roughly, "Don't try any of that nonsense. You and I are in this mess together."

The blow unloosed in her body a spasm of trembling. She sank to the floor, amazed, thinking, *Can I really let him do this to me? I should have him arrested.*

But she knew from the quailing inside her that she dared not.

"Tell me," he demanded, "has he *any* reason?"

As through a mist, Marie looked up at a man whose lean face glistened with perspiration. Dark eyes were narrowed, gleaming, not normal, long body was gaunt and rigid. With a shock, she realized that Walter had lost a lot of weight these past few weeks.

His entire aspect conveyed extreme subjectiveness and absorption with his own feelings, bringing conviction to her at some depth of her being that she was in severe danger.

All of this awareness came to her in flashes; not real thought at all, simply a sequence of feelings that in seconds eroded her resistance. Unable to stop herself, she spilled out to the accompaniment of uncontrollable tears the story of her one affair with Mac.

When she had finished, Walter walked over to a couch and sat down in it heavily. His cheeks had turned white. He mumbled at last, *"That's* a price I never expected to have to pay."

"The price you have to pay!" said Marie. "Have you gone crazy?"

As she climbed to her feet, she saw that he was shaking his head. The muscles on his face were so drawn that he almost looked like a stranger.

"Marie!" he croaked. "We're at basic. This is the full pressure."

"But Mac will never betray you!" she said. "You'll see. He's a good man."

Walter did an astonishing thing. He leaned over, lay down on the floor, and curled up like a baby. The uneasy thrill that came to Marie as she saw him do this yielded to confusion. Uncertainly, she walked forward, stooped over him, and said in a high-pitched voice, "Walter, what are you doing?"

A faint snore answered her. Unbelieving, she bent down and rolled him over.

He lay there sound asleep.

The truth hit her almost like another blow. This was basic fear.

She decided against calling Mac. About an hour later, when Walter stirred, she went over to him and shook him.

He sat up, stared at her, and then caught her hand, drew her down beside him, and began the preliminaries of lovemaking.

At first, it was too elemental a struggle for any sound but heavy breathing. Far in the back of her mind, as she fought, Marie had the wondering thought, *B-but he's impotent. How?*— After a minute more she had the further vague realization that the primitive forces released in this man had evidently broken through all such artificial barriers.

With an abrupt effort, she broke free of him and scrambled to her feet. Before she could flee, he was up, also, and had hold of her again.

Marie was able to gasp, "Walter, listen to me. Stop this foolishness!"

He whispered hoarsely, "We're in this murder together, Marie. I've got to make you realize that."

"Are you crazy? There's been no murder."

For a few moments it seemed as if that had penetrated. He released her. He gazed at her, eyes staring and vaguely puzzled. He said, "Marie, a woman involved in our predicament cannot be trusted with the wrong man."

With that he turned and walked to the door. Marie got there at the same time. "What are you going to do?" she asked.

He faced her. His eyes, gazing at her, held an odd, blank expression. Marie, who had parted her lips to speak, again closed them. For the first time it struck her, *This is his nervous breakdown.*

He seemed to forget her. He opened the door and walked out.

Marie let him go, for they were indeed at basic; and all the rest, she realized, was up to her.

As soon as Walter had gone, she changed her crumpled dress for a clean one and headed for the brain room. The time had come to find out what Carl had told Dr. MacKerrie.

CHAPTER IX

As she pressed the blue button a few minutes later, she was very determined. "Carl, can you receive me?"

"Marie, I've been thinking about what you told me— about your being ill a few days ago."

It took a moment to remember what he was talking

about: her excuse to him for not going near him while she was remaining indoors to avoid Mac.

She waited, stopped in her own purpose by his unexpected words. "Yes?" she said finally.

"I'm sorry to tell you that I don't believe you were ill. You just forgot about me."

"No, dear, that's not true," said Marie.

She was thinking impatiently that now they would have to waste time on this.

"It is characteristic of a woman," said Carl, "that she develops total contempt for an ineffectual male. I am now the most ineffectual male in human history, and you've already started neglecting me. Soon you'll have days on end when you won't even remember I'm here."

His words tied in with her purpose, and so she was able to say, "Communication between you and me is the very subject I want us to talk about. And so, my first question is, have you told Dr. MacKerrie any of your subjective feelings about our personal relationship?"

Silence; then he said, "That's a pointed question."

"Yes or no."

"Wait a minute. Let me think over what I've said."

The silence grew longer. As she waited, Marie found herself absently noticing the brain. There it lay in its transparent case, partly supported by another transparent structure. It was being held—she realized in that moment of keen observation—in exactly the position it would be in if it were inside his head and he were standing.

Even as she had the thought, she grew aware that she was actually looking at the brain. She gasped, started to turn away—and then stopped herself. Deliberately, she gazed at the monstrosity. And there it was: pink and gray, curly and folded in upon itself.

. . . The central switchboard of a human being; perhaps the very essence of humanness was there as well as all those neural mechanisms that now, under stress, were moving in such an uncontrolled fashion.

She'd have to get used to the idea that this was what was left of Carl, who, long ago, she had loved enough to marry, who, for nearly a year had been her sweetheart, and who had always been quite willing after she learned the truth to include her as one of his concubines. Indeed, he had once offered her all his Wednesday nights.

Her train of thought ended as Carl spoke again. "Yes," he said.

It took her several dozen heartbeats to remember what the question was that he had answered. Then, "What did you tell him?"

"That you and I had not had intimate relations for fourteen years."

"Oh!"

Carl's voice pleaded hastily, "Now look, dear, he's a doctor."

"But not *my* doctor," Marie said. She restrained her anger. "What else did you tell him?"

"Well—"

"Tell me!"

"Marie—" Pleading— "Please don't press me so hard. I'm not up to it. Remember, I'm alone here in this darkness. I need your sympathy and understanding, not your rage."

She let up slightly. "All right, my dear. But why don't you just tell me everything, and then we can start from there?"

"I'm ashamed of some of it."

"Tell me, please. Our future communication depends on complete honesty."

"All right, Marie. When I analyzed the hopelessness of my position, I pictured you out there, only thirty-eight years old, a beautiful woman, attractive to men—and I trapped here unable to do or see anything except through this damned machinery. For a while I was mad with jealous fear. I told Mac I thought Walter had killed me—"

So their worst fear was true. Marie felt a terrible inner grief.

Carl continued. "I'm still fairly sure that he did it. Because after you went away to visit your parents, I threatened Walter in a fashion that no real man would take from another man. You won't understand that because you're lost in a woman's mental machinery. But I provoked him, and I got what I should have known I would get. Jealousy is not a clever emotion. Stay away from Walter, Marie. He's a dangerous man."

Marie remembered Walter's sleeping figure on the floor
and shrugged. She became aware of the contempt in her
body gesture and had a sharp feeling of guilt that, after
a moment, she rejected. Walter had by his act indicated
that he expected her to solve his problem. In such a situation, guilt could not be a factor.

Carl was speaking again: "Marie, you're sure everything
is okay?"

"Yes, my dear," she lied.

"I don't understand it." Plaintively. "By my figuring, you
should be getting deeper into trouble every hour until—
wham!—the whole thing blows sky high."

He had never explained what he meant by the predicted
blowup. And Marie had never dared ask, for fear that the
slightest questioning on *that* subject would arouse his suspicion.

She thought, *That's all we'd need, to have Carl go into
a breakdown.*

Before she could say anything, Carl said apologetically,
"Marie, my dear, I have one more confession to make."

Momentarily, the word transfixed her; then, she said even-
ly, "Confession?"

"I guess," he continued darkly, "I've been torturing myself with all these thoughts about the inevitability of your
being made love to by other men, while I—well, you know,
here I am, helpless."

Marie dared not say a word for fear it would be the
wrong one.

"So," Carl said, "I pictured you a victim of male madness—which exists, Marie; don't misunderstand me. And
having my view of you as a prime innocent, I had you
practically already living the life of a prostitute.

"To be honest with you," Carl went on, "I was puzzled
as to how it would end. I had never carried the thought
beyond the woman's dilemma."

Marie waited, breathless.

Carl continued. "What worries me is that the only ending
I can imagine is some kind of crisis where you get killed.
It would probably have the appearance of suicide."

Immediately tears flowed from Marie's eyes.

During all these shattered weeks, somewhere in the depths
of her mind had been the feeling that she *was* doomed.

And now he had said it, also.

Carl was speaking again. "I can see I was wrong. I forgot my own rules. Every woman operates from an impregnable position. You may think, surely, a prostitute can't possibly justify her actions. But you're wrong. She does. In the same way, if you had actually been having an affair with Walter, you would be doing it in such a way that he could never find fault with your reason for doing so. What I've kept forgetting is that your impregnable position has been the strange purity of frigidity. A frigid woman in our society has the most impregnable moral status of all. But there has to be a reason why you became that way. As I see it now, the reason can only be rooted in the fact that, when you married me, it was for forever. What other reason can there be for your having remained faithful to me right to this minute? And I finally accept that you are. There, does that make you feel better?"

Marie sighed.

She presumed that now she had become pure again in his mind, there would come the inevitable offer of a joint suicide pact.

There was a long silence from the voice box; then he said, "Marie!"

"Yes, my dear?"

"Let me think about this, and please come back this evening. Will you do that? I have something very important to say to you."

What was amazing to Marie once more was the similarity to the past. Invariably, the cycle had been: jealousy, mad jealousy, acceptance of her purity, and then a grave statement of an important communication, which had always turned out to be a suicide offer. Carl never seemed to realize how stereotyped an emotional thing he did on such occasions. And each time he seemed to forget that he had done it before.

But she thought, *I'll come back. I'll listen.*

She promised him and departed.

CHAPTER X

About midafternoon, the first sharp alarm came.

Suicide! she thought. *Can that be* his *way of going into a nervous breakdown?*

The pattern had occurred so often, it had acquired in her mind a kind of normalcy—something to be patiently lived with.

But it wasn't normal. It was incredibly abnormal.

What appalled her was her own unawareness. The very reassurance she had given Carl—to calm him—had now produced the crisis.

Marie hurried back to the brain room and searched it for explosives—found nothing.

Next, she anxiously went over the list of objects, chemicals, and materials that Carl had ordered brought in from time to time, and she located and looked over each item in turn.

Nothing.

That is, nothing that would combine in any way to help a man commit suicide.

She sought out Mac and without giving any reason questioned him. His gentle face grew thoughtful. But in the end he shook his head.

"Only thing I can recall is that he asked me, a couple of years ago now, about what we planned to do with his brain after he died. I told him then, of course, as I told you that our plan was to keep as many scientists' brains alive as we could as long as we could. As you know, that hasn't worked out. We don't get there in time. But I'm sure—" he finished— "that Dr. Carl never imagined anything happening to him soon. And so it's unlikely that he made preparations."

Marie, remembering the numerous offers of suicide pacts, said thoughtfully, "He was obsessed with the whole concept of death. It was never far from his mind. Is there any way in which he could kill himself?"

But Mac was not the person of whom to ask such a question. He said tolerantly, "As things stand, Carl will probably live forever."

He hesitated, suddenly serious. "The fact makes it necessary for us all to make permanent decisions."

He broke off, said earnestly, "This is a hard world, Marie, and I'm as hard a man in some ways as any other. When I see a woman going the way you're going, I find in myself a determination to do what's necessary to stop it."

Marie shrank. "What do you mean?"

He said, "I hate to seem cruel, but I'm determined that you'll have to choose between Walter and me."

For some reason she could not bring herself to be angry with him. She brushed past him without a word.

Early evening.

She remembered the book of aphorisms.

She headed for Carl's room. First she ransacked the drawers of his desk, untouched up to now. Then she glanced along the shelves of his wardrobe, and finally she opened bureau drawers.

It was in the bureau that she found an address booklet. It was not what she was looking for. But she paused to glance through it at a formidable list of women's names and addresses. Altogether, she counted twenty-eight. Most had old dates notated beside them.

Presumably, these were discarded mistresses of yesteryears.

. . . Ann, Lil, Diane, Esther, Grace, June, Velvet—

Marie stopped. "Velvet!" she exclaimed scathingly.

She was impatiently shoving the little notebook back into the drawer when she saw the red glint of what she had come for.

Women Are Doomed.

Quickly clutching the volume, she hurried down the silent hall to her own apartment. She settled herself in a chair, turned the cover, and read the lone paragraph on page one:

The biggest unexplored universe is not out in space or on other stars or in far galaxies. It is right there between your two ears, my dear Marie.

Marie's lips tightened. She closed the little book with a snapping sound, and then, shrugging, gazed curiously at the hand-printed title on the cover. Underneath the title in longhand was written, "To be read by my wife, Dr. Marie Hazzard, only in the event of my demise. See page 2."

She had read page 1. Now she opened the book again. The second page also contained a single, though somewhat longer paragraph.

Naturally one cannot see the future in exact detail, but it has occurred to me that a person like myself may well meet a premature end at the hands of a jealous husband, or a rejected mistress, or even—God forbid, of course—by Marie, my long-suffering spouse. Who knows what has been going on these many betrayed years in that woman's noodle, least of all she herself would have no idea.

She thought, *Same old Carl, writing when he was at the peak of his destructiveness.*

She thereupon read every little negative gem in the book, almost with the feeling that Carl was saying it aloud; for she knew every line. There were no surprises. It had all been said many times over the years in Carl's sardonic voice, although a few of the items she had forgotten.

She had counted on learning from Carl's own words how to deal with Carl. And so, the realization that there was nothing new, and that she must depend on herself, was bitterly disappointing.

Disconsolate, she went out to the deserted lab and began those mechanical preparations that might be of some help in the purely physical realm but had no value in warding off the crisis and its consequences. Her first task was to set up a closed-circuit television between the brain room and a position near the outer door.

That was relatively easy to do, requiring mostly the pushing around of things that were a little too heavy for her. But the sets were available; the lab used television in building dangerous equipment with remote-controlled instruments.

Next, she installed a relay for pressing the blue button. And that was not so much difficult as it was time-consuming. There was nothing in the lab quite like what she needed to build it, and so she worked up a makeshift in the machine room from a few basic parts.

Shortly after ten-thirty she was ready.

As she stood at the door, taking a few breaths of fresh air, trying to recover from sustained physical effort, she remembered a promise she had made Walter . . . at the beginning: that she would never do anything about Carl without consulting him.

Her angry impulse was to reject the promise.

But after a moment's thought, she headed for Walter's cottage. She pressed the buzzer for a full minute before she used her master key.

She found him in a bottomless sleep in his bed. All her shaking could not awaken him.

Marie went out, shaking her head. It occurred to her that this was how Walter paid the "price"—in sleep, forgetfulness.

As she headed once more for the lab, she visualized Mac helplessly ill in his cottage, Walter in his virtual unconsciousness, and Carl like an automaton dramatizing the finale of his cyclic jealousy of her. Brilliant men in their fields; competent, skillful—

None of that applied here.

In an odd way it was reassuring. The very mechanicalness of it made for predictability.

Pointed to a kind of solution.

. . . If frigid Marie would unthaw, the men with bodies would maintain an uneasy truce, and the man without a body would, of course, continue his scheming.

Could Carl do anything?

That was what she had to find out before she confronted in all its stark meaning what she would do in a situation that had degenerated into an unseemly male battle for possession of her.

She entered the lab and turned a switch. Then, with a firm movement, she activated the relay that pressed down the blue button in the brain room more than a hundred feet away.

Watching the scene on the TV screen before her, she said, "Carl, here I am."

"Are we alone?"

"Yes." She added, "It's nearly eleven at night."

"Good. It's important that we be alone, dear. What I have to say is for your ears only."

As she had anticipated, he now proposed a suicide pact.

"It will bring us together in some other plane of existence, darling, where we can eternally be the true lovers we were destined to be." He continued. "What makes this so urgent, my dear, is the sad fact that purity doesn't last, not even in a good woman—"

Marie felt a great wonder. *Is this a basic male thing—this desire for chasteness in a woman?*

Clearly, of all men Carl was among those who had the least right to require purity in his woman. Yet this was what he was now in a panic about . . . There must be something in the male brain itself, a nerve center perhaps, that ceaselessly demanded that his woman belong only to him.

She realized that she had always sensed this need in Carl, and she had been extremely careful. That he had accused her anyway merely showed what a powerful, irrational force it was.

She realized it was time she spoke to him.

She said, "You don't have to worry, my dear. I'm not about to break out of my frigidity."

"But I'm right. You do love me?"

"No, dear, you're wrong. You lost my love long ago, remember?"

"You don't know your own truth, my sweet Marie. So I can see I have to decide for both of us."

"As you always did," said Marie.

But something in his voice set off an alarm reaction inside her. She thought anxiously, *He sounds as if he actually has something.*

She listened nervously as Carl went on:

"Marie, you probably know that no human being can long remain the way I am and not despair. And so, when Dr. MacKerrie used to talk about the possibility of keeping my brain and yours alive after death—remember, when he first came around. Anyway, I realized that I'd be pretty helpless if it ever happened. So, when he showed me how they would recreate my voice with analogs, I rigged up some relays that could be triggered by the sound of my voice alone—no one else's. I installed one inside the wall of every room in the laboratory. And, darling, please believe me when I say that what I'm going to do now will bring us together in some other plane, true lovers for all time. I'm sure you really want that, sweetheart, so—"

He broke off. "Don't run, dear. It's too late. You won't make it outside in time. Good-by, darling, see you in the hereafter—"

As she ran across the garden, Marie heard Carl's voice on the TV beyond the wall yell something—undoubtedly the signal.

The mechanism he had set up must have operated through some lag of its own. Because she was actually safe beside the house itself when an explosion rocked the end of the laboratory where the brain room was located.

A blast of wind rushed past her.

Marie stood, then, watching the growing fire.

CHAPTER XI

At first she was blank.

After a while she realized that a crowd was gathering. In the distance there was the sound of a fire engine.

An instant later—it seemed—nine great engines roared up one after another. Uniformed men hurried past her.

Marie scarcely saw them.

She was having a fantasy.

In her mind's eye, she saw both Walter and Mac in their separate cottages; they had their suitcases open, and they were packing.

So vivid was the imagined picture that she thought, *The nightmare is over, and those who made it a nightmare know that their game is over, too.*

She had a sudden qualm about Walter. Had he been a victim along with her?

She couldn't be sure, but she thought not.

Everyone involved had realized at some level of their being that she was the one that was vulnerable.

And they had moved in on her. Without mercy they had forced her.

Mentally, she wrote a letter to Bob Lindley dismissing him as her attorney. And her lips were framing the savage words she would use to Mac and Walter—when she became aware that Dr. MacKerrie had come up beside her.

"Marie, my dear," he said solicitously, "I have a sedative here for you. How awful this must be for you—"

Marie pulled away violently as she heard his voice. The shock memory came of what Carl had said. ". . . Appearance of suicide—"

She pictured the death notice: *Overdose of sleeping medicine!*

Aloud, she snapped, "Take your own damned sedative!"

She dodged as he grabbed at her and darted off through the crowd. As she ran, she heard MacKerrie's voice, high-pitched, tense, desperate. "Hold that woman! She's become hysterical."

Someone grabbed her and held her. She looked up into Walter's eyes. "Marie," he said sadly, "what's the matter with you?"

There was such a strange expression in his eyes that Marie shrank. "Walter," she begged, "for God's sake, Walter, don't kill me."

His grip on her tightened, and he placed his hand over her mouth. "It's all right, my dear, it's only a sedative." He raised his voice. "Dr. Mac, come over here. She's in a bad way."

She thought, *Doesn't he realize? If Mac kills me, then two people will know about my murder!*

Deep inside, Marie began to laugh. She thought, *Carl, Carl, I've really got to hand it to you. You did understand human beings.*

Abruptly, she bit Walter's hand as hard as she could. And gave him a shove with every bit of her strength.

It was like pushing at a wall. He held her. "Marie!" he said chidingly. "Marie."

Dr. MacKerrie came up. She felt the needle sink into her arm.

As she drifted into unconsciousness, she heard her bewildered voice say, "But how did you both know? So quickly? Each separately? And why?"

Why had it become necessary to destroy her? And by what logic had each of them known it? Was it a male understanding?

It was awful to die and not know the reason.

These were the thoughts that she carried into the blackness.

CHAPTER XII

She came to.

Joy.

I'm alive, she thought. *Oh, God, I'm still alive.*

Marie opened her eyes and looked up into the kindly face of Dr. MacKerrie. Her gaze flashed beyond him, and she saw that she was in her own bedroom and that it was daylight. After bare instants she looked at Mac once more, and now she was cringing.

Dr. MacKerrie said, "Marie, that frightened expression is on your face again. Relax. There's nothing to be afraid of. Walter and I covered up for you completely."

She heard only the first part of his statement; of his ending words, the reassurance came through, nothing else.

She began to feel not safe but safer.

Abruptly she asked, "Covered up what?"

He bent down like a conspirator and said in a low voice, "The explosion brought Walter and me outside, and I guess we both saw right away what you had done— I should have realized when you were questioning me this afternoon that this whole thing was getting too much for you."

There must have been a frightened look on her face, for he said quickly, "Everything is okay. You'll see."

Marie, who had been about to deny that there was anything to cover up, almost bit her lip in her effort to remain silent.

Finally she asked, "How did you cover up?"

It turned out that they had removed the remote-control

apparatus and the closed-circuit TV before the firemen got there.

"The one in Carl's room was pretty well banged up," Mac reported. "So we shoved that into the junk room. And when I talked to Carl—"

Marie galvanized. "Carl!" she gasped.

"You forgot about that metal roof he had rigged over the brain," said Mac soothingly. "It diverted the full force of the explosion. It's almost as if he anticipated the direction from which it would come. Anyway, he promised he would say nothing."

Marie, lying there, grimly made up an aphorism of her own: "The kind of a man who offers his sweetheart a joint suicide pact usually has a good aim when he's firing at her and a poor aim for himself."

She grew very angry. *Oh, he promised that, did he?* But she didn't say it aloud.

There were too many mixed emotions and uncertainties in her for speech.

It was clear now that Walter and Mac believed that they had saved her the night before from inadvertently revealing that she had tried to commit murder.

What was shocking was that the two men had teamed up to save her. Could that have a special significance?

She gazed up at Mac. "What are you planning to do?" she asked huskily.

"You'll get no more one-sided arguments from me," he answered. "You've convinced me."

But of what? Marie thought. *Of what?*

Now that she knew Carl was alive, she felt vulnerable. But to what extent, she couldn't decide. There was certainly no sign of Mac leaving.

"Where's Walter?" she whispered.

"He's waiting outside. I'll send him in." He bent and kissed her on the lips. "Don't worry. You can have your cake and eat it, too."

A minute later the door opened. Walter came in. He sank down beside the bed, and a slow smile came over his face.

"I've got to hand it to you," he said. "It sure would have solved your problem, wouldn't it?"

Marie gazed at him, infinite hostility in her eyes.

"But," said Walter, "after what he said to me that night

when he accused me, I'd rather he remained in this condition, alive, unable to function. So even though it was dangerous to me to have him like this, I never planned any further attack on him myself."

For Marie, resentment yielded to puzzlement. She couldn't quite decide what he was trying to say.

Walter continued. "When I realized that even my being impotent didn't protect you from other men—I just waited my opportunity and ran him down."

Marie felt her body contract under the sheets. "Why are you admitting this to me?" she breathed.

Walter explained. "Now, we're in the same box. It's a little hard to imagine either of us giving the other away."

So he wasn't leaving, either.

"Have you told Mac?" she asked.

"Don't worry about Mac. After last night he and I had to come to an understanding."

He shook his head, amazed. "You really forced this thing to a rapid conclusion. Trust a woman," he said tolerantly.

Marie, who had been forced into every move, felt keenly the futility of any words.

Walter continued. "Just think, yesterday I was at the stage where I was merely toying with the idea of making love to Carl's wife. Remember?"

Marie recalled the desperate battle that she had won.

Walter said, "I felt it would give me a lot of satisfaction —after the way Carl accused me. I decided I didn't want any part of it, on thinking it over during the afternoon. And then—"

He spread his hands, grinning.

"After that thing last night, Mac insisted that I agree that he and I share you."

There was a pause. Marie shrank. "Mac agreed to *that?*" she said.

Walter's eyes glistened as he stared at her. "The way I look at it," he said softly, "you've got some feeling for this man. I don't know just how or what, but there's something. I figure you can go for this guy."

She was beginning to recover, to gird herself. Walter must have seen the look, for he held up his hand hastily. "Wait!" he said. "I could see right away that Mac was

133

in some big emotion, and of course I realized you wouldn't stand for it, and besides—"

He paused for a moment, then continued: "I'm afraid my dear wife turned me against women who are having affairs with other men."

He stopped. His expression hardened. "But I can't let Mac know that. So this is *our* agreement—yours and mine —he gets you, but don't you ever let on that I haven't got you, also. If you do—"

"What will you do?" Marie spoke in a low voice.

Walter's eyes were narrowed slits. "I'll say that you and I were lovers. I'll say that we planned Carl's murder. I'll swear that you coaxed me into it. I'll—"

He stopped. He swallowed hard. "*Get it!*" he said from between clenched teeth.

Marie seemed to be gazing at him as from a distance. There was a mist over her eyes, like clouds, hiding remote objects. She could not possibly have uttered a word, but she was remembering one of the aphorisms she had read in Carl's book.

"It takes a lot of energy for a man to get a frigid female into bed and progressively more energy for him to keep her there. But every once in a while such a woman maneuvers herself into an emotional cul-de-sac whereby she has no alternative. I keep trying to figure out how I can work this swindle on Marie. But I can't even imagine the energy that would do it."

CHAPTER XIII

It was a month later.

She woke up; and there was the anger. Marie lay very still, conscious of her flushed skin and of a hard core of something inside her, a mixture of resentful thought and emotion, a feeling of resistance, a tense yet helpless condition of muscular rigidity. It was the anger of a prisoner, of a trapped being, and yes—she thought—of a slave.

A slave must never show anger even when abused.

Marie dressed impatiently. As she made up her face, she tried for the first time to relax the taut, drawn muscles around her mouth.

She thought uneasily, *I'd better be careful. If I lose my looks, I'll cease to be attractive, and Mac will leave me. And then who knows what will happen?*

The realization had welled up so casually that a long moment passed before she grasped the full implication. Then—

"Oh, my lord."

Ironically, she must use all the known feminine devices for keeping the situation exactly as it was: beauty aids, beauty parlors, masseurs.

The trap was as perfect as that.

After a short, bitter consideration of the reality, she leafed through the yellow pages, found the phone number of a beauty specialty shop in Beverly Hills, and made an appointment for the following morning.

She went next to research and examined the progress that was being made on certain problems. Each item of custom equipment presented special difficulties of construction.

Walter came up beside her. He said, "We'll have to ask Carl about this one."

Marie watched his face as he explained the difficulty in technical terms. He was so calm, so objective, so accepting of the whole situation.

She thought wonderingly, *Why do I keep being so disturbed by the situation? Nobody else seems to worry.*

She listened to the problem as he outlined it, saw what it was he was not observing in it—why the field would not reverse under conditions of superconductivity—and nodded quietly, saying, "I'll ask Carl."

These days she never volunteered solutions herself. That was a man's world.

The hum of activity in the lab was abruptly silenced as she closed the door of the soundproof brain room behind her.

Mac was there.

He turned as she entered and waved at her cheerfully. "Everything dandy here!" he said. "Healthiest brain in the world. At this rate he'll outlive all of us. Want to talk to him alone?"

"Yes."

Mac headed for the door but paused on the threshold. "See you tonight?" he asked.

"Of course."

Her voice held a bare edge of sharpness in it. What else? There was no escape for her.

But she turned and watched him leave, suddenly curious. He walked out of the room, head back, apparent acceptance in every movement and muscle in his strong surgeon's body.

He had assigned his relationship with her to Mondays, Wednesdays, and Fridays. On the other nights, he left the grounds early and stayed away till noon the following day.

It was his belief, of course, that she spent Tuesday, Thursday, Saturday, and Sunday nights with Walter. But it was interesting that he had not once stayed around to find out that it was not so.

His absence seemed to be a continuing evidence that Walter's presence was still a knife painfully buried in a vital spot in Mac.

Marie thought, *That's all the pleasure I have out of this: that he's in some kind of small agony.*

As she pressed the button, she could feel the tense anger deep inside her, unchanged by all her rationalizations.

Exactly like yesterday.

And the day and week before.

She thought, *I'm as lost as Carl.*

So were Walter and Mac.

They were all moving through space together. Somewhere out beyond the orbit of Mars, at least.

Heading into the great night of the universe.

LOST: FIFTY SUNS

I

THE STREET loud-speaker clattered into life. A man's voice said resonantly:

"Attention, citizens of the planets of the Fifty Suns. This is the Earth battleship *Star Cluster*. In a few moments, the Right Honorable Gloria Cecily, Lady Laurr of Noble Laurr, Grand Captain of the *Star Cluster,* will make an announcement."

Maltby, who had been walking toward an airlift car, stopped as the voice sounded from the radio. He saw that other people were pausing, also.

Lant was a new planet for him; its capital city was delightfully rural after the densely populated Cassidor, where the Fifty Suns Space Navy had its main base. His own ship had landed the day before, on general orders commanding all warships to seek refuge immediately on the nearest inhabited planet.

It was an emergency order, with panic implicit in it. From what he had heard at officers' mess, it was clear that it had something to do with the Earth ship whose broadcast was now being transmitted over the general-alarm system.

On the radio, the man's voice said impressively, "And here is Lady Laurr."

A young woman's clear, firm silvery voice began, "People of the Fifty Suns, we *know* you are there.

"For several years my ship the *Star Cluster* has been mapping the Greater Magellanic Cloud. Accidentally, we ran into one of your space meteorological stations and captured its attendant. Before he succeeded in killing himself, we learned that somewhere in this cloud of about a hundred million stars, there are fifty inhabited sun systems with a total of seventy planets with human beings living on them.

"It is our intention to find you, though it may seem at first thought that it will be impossible for us to do so. Locating fifty suns scattered among a hundred million stars seems difficult in a purely mechanical way. But we have devised a solution to the problem that is only partly mechanical.

"Listen well now, people of the Fifty Suns. We know who you are. We know that you are the Dellian and non-Dellian robots—so-called; not really robots at all, but flesh-and-blood humanoids. And, in looking through our history books, we have read about the foolish riots of fifteen thousand years ago that frightened you and made you leave the main galaxy and seek sanctuary far away from human civilization.

"Fifteen thousand years is a long time. Men have changed. Such unpleasant incidents as your ancestors experienced are no longer possible. I say this to you in order to ease your fears. Because you must come back into the fold. You must join the Earth galactic union, subscribe to certain minimum regulations, and establish interstellar commercial ports.

"Because of your special reasons for concealing yourselves, you are allowed one sidereal week to reveal to us the location of your planets. During that time we shall take no action. After that time, for each sidereal day that passes without contact being established, there will be a penalty.

"Of this you may be sure. We shall find you. And quickly!"

The speaker was silent, as if to let the meaning of the words sink in. Near Maltby, a man said, "Only one ship. What are we afraid of? Let's destroy it before it can go back to the galaxy and report our presence."

A woman said uneasily, "Is she telling the truth, or is she bluffing? Does she really believe they can locate us?"

A second man spoke gruffly. "It's impossible. It's the old needle in the haystack problem, only worse."

Maltby said nothing, but he was inclined to agree. It

seemed to him that Grand Captain Laurr, of the Earth ship, was whistling in the greatest darkness that had ever hidden a civilization.

On the radio, the Right Honorable Gloria Cecily was speaking again:

"In the event that you do not keep time the way we do, a sidereal day is made up of twenty hours of a hundred minutes each day. There are a hundred seconds in a minute, and in that second light travels 100,000 miles exactly. Our day is somewhat longer than the old-style day in which a minute was sixty seconds and light-speed 186,300-odd miles a second.

"Govern yourselves accordingly. One week from today I shall call again."

There was a pause. And then the voice of a man—not the one who had introduced the woman—said:

"Citizens of the Fifty Suns, that was a transcribed message. It was delivered about an hour ago and was re-broadcast on the instructions of the Fifty Suns council in accordance with our desire to keep the populace abreast of all developments in this, the most serious danger that has ever threatened us.

"Continue about your daily business and be assured that everything possible is being done. Further information will be given out as it is received.

"That is all for now."

Maltby climbed aboard the airlift car, which settled down at his signal. As he sank into a vacant seat, a woman came over and sat down beside him. He felt the faintest tugging sensation at his mind. His eyes widened a little, but he gave no other sign that he had felt the probing of the woman spy's mind.

She said after a little, "Did you hear the broadcast?"

"Yes."

"What did you think of it?"

"The commander seemed very positive."

"Did you notice that she had identified all of us here in the Fifty Suns as Dellian and non-Dellian robots?"

He was not surprised that she had got it, also. The Earth people did not know that there was a third group in the Fifty Suns—the mixed men. For thousands of years after the migration, a Dellian and non-Dellian marriage had not produced children. Finally, by what was known as the cold-pressure system, children became possible. The result was the so-called Mixed Man, with two minds, Dellian physical strength and non-Dellian creative ability. The two minds, properly coordinated, could dominate any person who had only one mind.

Maltby was a Mixed Man. So was the woman sitting beside him, as he had recognized from the way she had momentarily stimulated his brain. The difference between them was, he had a legal status on Lant and other planets of the Fifty Suns. She didn't. If she were caught, she would be subject to imprisonment or death.

"We've been following you," she said, "intending to contact you ever since our headquarters heard this message something over an hour ago. What do you think we should do?"

Maltby hesitated. It was hard for him to accept his role of hereditary leader of the Mixed Men; he who was also a captain in the Fifty Suns space fleet. Twenty years before, the Mixed Men had tried to seize control of the Fifty Suns. The attempt had ended in disastrous failure, as a result of which they were declared outlaws. Maltby, then a small boy, had been captured by a Dellian patrol party. The fleet educated him. He was an experiment. It was recognized that the problem of the Mixed Men would have to be solved. A prolonged effort was made to teach him loyalty to the Fifty Suns as a whole; and to a considerable extent it was a success. What his teachers didn't know was that they had in their power the nominal leader of the Mixed Men.

It had put a conflict into Maltby's mind, one which he had not yet resolved. He said slowly, "At the moment my feeling is that we should automatically stick with the group. Let us act openly with the Dellians and non-Dellians. After all, we, too, are of the Fifty Suns."

The woman said, "There has already been talk of the possibility that we could gain some advantage by giving away the location of one of the planets."

For a moment, despite his own ambivalent training, that shocked Maltby. And yet he could see what she meant. The situation was alive with dynamic potentialities. He thought ruefully, *I guess I'm not temperamentally suited for in-*

trigue. He grew calmer, more thoughtful, more prepared to discuss the problem objectively. "If Earth located this civilization and recognized its government, then no changes would be possible. Any plans we might have for altering the situation in our favor—"

The woman—she was a slim blonde—smiled grimly, a savage light in her blue eyes. "If we gave them away," she said, "we could make the condition that we would hereafter receive equal status. That's all we want, basically."

"Is it?" Maltby knew better, and he was not pleased. "I seem to remember the war we waged had other purposes."

"Well—" The woman was defiant. "Who has a better right to the dominant position? We are physiologically superior to the Dellians and non-Dellians. For all we know, we may be the only super-race in the Galaxy." She broke off tensely. "There's another, greater possibility: These Earth people have never run into Mixed Men. If we had the advantage of surprise—if we could get enough of our people aboard their ship—we might capture new, decisive weapons. Do you see?"

Maltby saw many things, including the fact that there was a great deal of wishful thinking involved. "My dear," he said, "we are a small group. Our revolution against the Fifty Suns government failed despite initial surprise. It is possible that we might be able to do all these things, given time. But our ideas are bigger than our numbers."

"Hunston thinks the time to act is during a crisis."

"Hunston!" said Maltby involuntarily.

And then he was silent.

Alongside the colorful and demanding Hunston, Maltby felt himself drab. His was the unpopular role of holding in check the fierce passions of undisciplined young people. Through his followers, mostly elderly men, friends of his dead father, he could do nothing but advocate caution. It had proved a thankless task. Hunston was a subleader of the Mixed Men. His dynamic program of action now appealed to the younger people, to whom the disaster of the previous generation was mere hearsay. Their attitude was, "The leaders then made mistakes. We won't."

Maltby himself had no desire for dominance over the people of the Fifty Suns. For years he had asked himself the question, "How can I direct the ambitions of the Mixed

Men into less belligerent channels?" Up to now he had found no ready solution. He said slowly, firmly, "When the group is threatened, the ranks must close. Whether we like it or not, we are of the Fifty Suns. It may be that it would be advisable to betray this civilization to Earth, but that is not something for us to decide an hour after the opportunity presents itself. Advise the hidden cities that I want three days of discussion and free criticism. On the fourth day there will be a plebiscite on which the issue will be: betray, or not betray? That is all."

From the corner of his eye he saw that the woman was not pleased. Her face was suddenly sullen; there was suppressed anger in the way she held herself.

"My dear," he said gently, "surely you are not thinking in terms of going against the majority?"

He could see, then, from her changing expression that he had started the old democratic conflicts in her mind. It was his great hold on all these people, the fact that the Mixed Men council—of which he was head—appealed on all major issues directly to the group. Time had proved that plebiscites brought out the conservative instincts of a people. Individuals who for months had talked angrily of the forthright steps that must be taken grew cautious when confronted by a plebiscite ballot. Many a dangerous political storm had blown itself out in the ballot box.

The woman, who had been silent, said slowly, "In four days some other group may have decided to do the betraying; and we will have lost the advantage. Hunston thinks that in a crisis government should act without delay. Later, it can ask the people if they think its action was correct."

For that at least Maltby had an adequate answer. "The fate of an entire civilization is involved. Shall one man or a small group commit, first, a few hundred thousand of their own people and, through them, sixteen billion citizens of the Fifty Suns? I think not. But now, here is where I get off. Good luck."

He stood up and presently climbed to the ground. He did not look back as he headed for the steel barrier beyond which was one of several small bases that the Fifty Suns Military Forces maintained on the planet of Lant.

The guard at the gate examined his credentials with a frown and then said in a formal tone, "Captain, I have orders to escort you to the Capitol building, where local government leaders are in conference with military commanders. Will you come peaceably?"

Outwardly, Maltby did not hesitate. "Of course," he said.

A minute later, he was in a military air car being flown back across the city.

It was not as yet, he recognized, an inescapable situation. In an instant he could concentrate his two minds in a certain pattern and control first his guard and then the pilot of the craft.

He decided to do neither. It struck him that a conference of government leaders did not spell immediate danger for Captain Peter Maltby. Indeed, he could expect to learn something.

The small ship landed in a courtyard between two ivy-covered buildings. Maltby was taken through a door into a broad, brightly lighted corridor and so was ushered into a room where a score of men sat around a conference table. His arrival had evidently been announced, for no one was talking as he entered. He glanced swiftly along the line of faces that turned toward him. Two he knew personally. Both wore the uniform of commanding officers of the fleet. Both nodded greeting. He acknowledged the recognition in each case with a nod of his own.

All the other men, including four men in uniform, he had not previously seen in person. He recognized several local government leaders and several local officers. It was easy to distinguish the Dellian from the non-Dellian. The former were, without exception, fine, handsome, strong-looking men. The latter varied widely. It was a pudgy non-Dellian at the head of the table facing the door who stood up. Maltby recognized him from news photos as Andrew Craig, a local government minister. "Gentlemen," Craig began, "let us not be evasive with Captain Maltby."

He addressed himself to Maltby. "Captain, a number of conversations have been in progress in connection with the threat of the so-called Earth battleship whose woman commander a short time ago made the announcement you probably heard."

Maltby inclined his head. "I heard it."

"Good. Here is the situation. It has already been more or less decided that we shall not reveal ourselves to this intruder regardless of inducements offered. A few people argued that now that the Earth has come to the Greater Magellanic Cloud discovery is inevitable sooner or later. But the time interval involved could be thousands of years. Our attitude is, let us stick together now and refuse contact. During the next decade—and it will take that long—we can send expeditions to the main galaxy and see just what is going on there. Having done that, we can then make our final decision on the matter of establishing relations. You can see that this is the sensible course."

He paused and gazed expectantly at Maltby. There was in his manner a hint of anxiety. Maltby said in an even tone, "That is undoubtedly the sensible course."

An audible sigh of relief went up from several men.

"However," Maltby continued, "can you be sure that some group or planet will not reveal our location to the Earth ship? Many people, many planets, have individual interests."

"Of that," said the pudgy man, "we are well aware. Which is why you have been invited to this meeting."

Maltby wasn't sure that it had been precisely an invitation, but he made no comment.

The spokesman went on. "We have now received communications from all Fifty Sun governments. They are uniformly agreed that we must remain hidden. But all are equally aware that unless we can obtain an agreement from the Mixed Men not to take advantage of this situation, then our unity will have been in vain."

For some minutes Maltby had guessed what was coming. And he had recognized it as a crisis in the relationship between Mixed Men and the people of the Fifty Suns. It was also, he saw clearly, a personal crisis for himself. He said, "Gentlemen, I have an idea that I am going to be asked to make contact with other Mixed Men. As a captain in the Fifty Suns military arm, any such contact will place me immediately in a very difficult position."

Vice-admiral Dreehan, commanding officer of the battleship *Atmion,* of which Maltby was assistant astrogator and chief meteorologist, spoke up. "Captain, you may agree freely to any proposal here made to you. Have no fear that your anomalous position is not appreciated."

"I should like," said Maltby, "to have that written into the minutes and note taken."

Craig nodded at the stenographers. "Please note!" he said.

"Proceed," said Maltby.

"As you have guessed," Craig went on, "we want you to convey our proposals to the—" He paused, scowling a little, obviously reluctant to use a word that lent an aura of legitimacy to the outlaw group—"to the governing council of the Mixed Men. You have, we believe, opportunity to make such a contact."

"Years ago," acknowledged Maltby, "I informed my commanding officer that I had been approached by emissaries of the Mixed Men and that permanent facilities for liaison existed on each planet of the Fifty Suns. It was decided at that time not to show any awareness of the existence of these agencies, as they would obviously go underground in a more thorough fashion—that is, they would not advise me of their future location."

Actually, the decision for him to inform the armed forces of the Fifty Suns that such agencies existed had been made by the plebiscite of the Mixed Men. It was felt that contact would be suspected and therefore should be admitted. It was further believed that the Fifty Suns would not molest the agencies except in an emergency. The action had proved soundly based. But here was the emergency.

"Frankly," said the pudgy man, "it is our conviction that the Mixed Men are going to regard this situation as one which strengthens their bargaining position." He meant political blackmail, and it was a significant commentary on the situation that he did not say so. "I am empowered," Craig went on, "to offer limited citizenship rights, access to certain planets, eventual right to live in cities—with the whole problem of legal and political rights to be taken up every ten years, with assurance that each time—depending on behavior during the previous decade—further privileges will be granted."

He paused, and Maltby saw that everyone was looking at him with a kind of tense eagerness. A Dellian politician broke the silence. "What do you think of it?"

Maltby sighed. Before the arrival of the Earth ship, it would have been a remarkable offer. It was the old story of a concession made under pressure at a time when those

145

who made it no longer controlled the situation. He said as much, not aggressively but with a to-the-point candor. Even as he spoke, he thought over the terms, and it seemed to him that they were sound and honest. Knowing what he knew of the ambitions of certain groups among the Mixed Men, it seemed to him that further concessions would be as dangerous to them as to their peaceable neighbors. In view of the past there had to be restrictions and a period of probation. Therefore, he tended to support the proposals, while recognizing that it would be hard, under the circumstances, to put them over. He made his point quietly and finished: "We'll just have to wait and see."

There was a brief silence after he had spoken; and then a heavy-faced non-Dellian said harshly, "My own feeling is that we're wasting our time in this cowardly by-play. Although the Fifty Suns have been at peace for a long time, we still have more than a hundred battleships in service, not counting a host of smaller craft. Out there somewhere in space is one Earth battleship. I say, let's send the fleet to destroy it! That way we'll eliminate every human being who knows we exist. Ten thousand years may go by before they accidentally discover us again."

Vice-admiral Dreehan said, "We've discussed that. The reason it is inadvisable is very simple: The Earth people may have new weapons which could defeat us. We can't take the chance."

"I don't care what weapons one ship has," said the other flatly. "If the navy does its duty, all our problems will be solved by a single decisive action."

Craig said curtly, "That is a last resort." He faced Maltby again. "You may tell the Mixed Men that if they turn down our offer, we do have a large fleet to use against the intruder. In other words, if they should pursue the course of betrayal, it would not necessarily gain them anything. You may go, Captain."

II

Aboard the Earth battleship, *Star Cluster*, Grand Captain, the Right Honorable Gloria Cecily, Lady Laurr of Noble Laurr, sat at her desk on the bridge, gazed out into space, and considered her situation.

In front of her was a multiplanal viewport set at full transparency. Beyond was blackness with, here and there, stars. Magnification was at zero, and so only a few stars were visible, with occasional splotches of light to indicate the star density in that direction. The biggest and blurriest haze was to her left: the main galaxy, of which Earth was one planet of one system, one grain of sand in a cosmic desert.

The woman scarcely noticed. For years some variation of that fantastic scene had been part of her life. She saw it and ignored it in the same moment. She smiled now, a smile of decision; pressed a button. A man's face came on to the plate in front of her. She said without preamble, "I have been informed, Captain, that there is disgruntlement at our decision to remain in the Greater Magellanic Cloud and search for the Fifty Suns civilization."

The Captain hesitated, then said carefully, "Your excellency, I have heard that your determination to make this search does not meet with universal approval."

His changing of her phrase "our decision" to "your determination" did not escape her.

The man went on. "Naturally, I cannot speak for all the members of the crew, since there are thirty thousand of them."

"Naturally," she said. And there was irony in her tone.

The officer seemed not to hear. "It seems to me, your excellency, that it might be a good idea to hold a general ballot on this matter."

"Nonsense. They'd all vote to go home. After ten years in space, they've become jellyfish. They have little mind and no purpose. Captain—" Her voice was soft, but there was a glint in her eyes— "I sense in your tone and bearing a

147

sort of emotional agreement with this—this childish instinct of the group. Remember, the oldest law of space flight is that someone must have the will to go forward. Officers are selected with the utmost care because they must not give in to this blind desire to go home. It has been established that people who finally do rush madly to their planet, and their house, have a momentary emotional satisfaction and then restlessly join up for another long voyage. We are too far from our galaxy to cater to such juvenile lack of discipline."

The officer said quietly, "I am familiar with these arguments."

"I am glad to hear it," said Grand Captain Laurr acidly. And broke the connection between them.

Next, she called Astrogation. A young officer answered. To him she said, "I want a series of orbits plotted that will take us through the Greater Magellanic Cloud in the quickest possible time. Before we're through, I want us to have been within five hundred light-years of every star in the system."

Some of the color faded from the youthful officer's face. "Your excellency," he gasped, "that is the most remarkable order that we have ever received. This cloud of stars is six thousand light-years in diameter. What velocity did you have in mind, remembering that we have no knowledge of the location of the storms here?"

The boy's reaction disconcerted her in spite of herself. Just for an instant she felt doubt. She had a brief abstract awareness of how great a volume of space she contemplated passing through.

The doubt passed. She stiffened herself. "I believe," she said, "that the density of storm areas in this system would limit us to about one light-year every thirty minutes."

She broke off curtly. "Have your chief advise me when these orbits have been completed."

"Yes, your excellency," said the young man. His voice was drab.

She broke that connection, sat back and manipulated a switch that altered the viewport in front of her into a reflecting surface. She stared at her image. She saw a slim, grim-faced, rather handsome young woman of thirty-five. The image was smiling faintly, ironically, an indication of her satisfaction with the two steps she had taken. The word would spread. People would begin to realize what she contemplated. There would be despair, then acceptance. She felt no regret. She had done what she had because she took it for granted that the governments of the Fifty Suns would not reveal the location of a single one of their planets.

She ate lunch alone on the bridge, feeling intense excitement. A struggle for control of the ship's destiny was imminent; and she knew that she must be prepared for every eventuality. Three calls came through before she had finished eating. She had set up an automatic busy signal; and so she ignored them. The busy signal meant, "I'm here, but don't bother me unless it's urgent." Each time the calls ceased within seconds.

After lunch she lay down for a while to sleep and think. Presently, she rose, walked over to a matter transmitter, made the necessary adjustments—and stepped through to Psychology House half a mile away.

Lieutenant Neslor, the chief psychologist and a woman, emerged from a nearby room and greeted her warmly. The Grand Captain outlined her problems. The older woman nodded and said:

"I thought you'd be down to see me. If you'll wait a moment, I'll turn my patient over to an assistant; and then I'll talk to you."

By the time she returned, Lady Laurr had felt an incidental curiosity. "How many patients do you have here?"

The older woman's gray eyes studied her thoughtfully. "My staff does about eight hundred hours of therapy a week."

"With your facilities that sounds tremendous."

Lieutenant Neslor nodded. "It's been on the increase for several years."

Lady Gloria shrugged and was about to dismiss the matter when another thought struck her. "What's the trouble?" she asked. "Homesickness?"

"I suppose you could call it that. We have several technical names for it." She broke off. "Now, don't you be too critical. This is a hard life for people whose work is purely routine. Big though the ship is, with each passing year its facilities are less satisfying to the individual."

The Right Honorable Gloria Cecily parted her lips to

say that her own work was routine, also. Just in time she realized that the remark would sound false, even condescending. Nevertheless, she shook her head impatiently. "I don't understand. We have everything aboard this ship. Equal numbers of men and women, endless activities, food in plenty, and more entertainment than a person could desire in an entire lifetime. You can walk under growing trees beside ever-running streams. You can get married and divorced, though of course no children are allowed. There are gay bachelors aboard, and bachelor girls. Everyone has a room of his own and the knowledge that his pay is accumulating and that he can retire at the end of the voyage." She frowned. "And right now, with the discovery of this civilization of the Fifty Suns the voyage should be very stimulating."

The older woman smiled. "Gloria, dear, you're not being very bright. It's stimulating to you and me because of our special positions. Personally, I'm looking forward to seeing how these people think and act. I've read up on the history of the so-called Dellian and non-Dellian robots, and there's a whole new world of discovery here—for me; but not for the man who cooks my meals."

The Grand Captain's face was determined again. "I'm afraid he'll just have to stick it out. And now, let's get to business. We've got a two-level problem: Keeping control of the ship. Finding the Fifty Suns. In that order, I think."

Their discussion lasted well into the main sleep period. In the end Lady Laurr returned to the bridge and to her apartment, which adjoined it, convinced that both problems were, as she had suspected, predominantly psychological.

The week of grace went by uneventfully.

At the precise hour that it ended, the Grand Captain called into council the divisional captains of her giant ship. And with her first words struck at the heart of the emotional tension she had divined was in the officers as well as the men. "As I see it, ladies and gentlemen, we must stay here until we find this civilization, even if it means remaining for another ten years."

The captains looked at their neighbors and stirred uneasily. There were thirty of them, all except four being men.

The Right Honorable Gloria Cecily Laurr of Noble Laurr went on. "Taking that into account, accepting the fact that long-run strategies are in order, has anyone a plan of proce-dure?"

Captain Wayless, chief of staff of the flight command, said, "I am personally opposed to the notion that this search should be continued."

The Grand Captain's eyes narrowed. She guessed from the expressions of the others that Wayless was stating a more generally held opinion than she had suspected. She said as quietly as had he, "Captain, there are procedures for overruling a ship's commanding officer. Why not follow one of them?"

Captain Wayless was pale. "Very well, your excellency," he said. "I invoke clause 492 of the Regulations."

In spite of herself, his prompt acceptance of her chal-lenge shocked her. She knew the clause, since it was a limitation of her own power. No one could possibly know all the regulations governing the minutiae of personnel con-trol. But she had learned that each individual knew the regulations relating to himself. When it came to personal rights, everyone was a space-lawyer, herself included.

But she sat now, white-faced, as Captain Wayless read the clause in a resonant voice: "Limitation . . . circum-stances justify the captains in council . . . a majority . . . two-thirds. . . . Original purpose of voyage . . ."

It was all there, as she recalled it, invoked against her now for the first time. The *Star Cluster* had been sent on a mapping expedition. The task was completed. In insisting on a change of purpose, she had brought her actions within the meaning of the regulation.

She waited till Wayless had put down the book. Then she said in a mild tone, "How do we vote?"

It was twenty-one against her and five for her. Four of-ficers abstained. Captain Dorothy Sturdevant, who headed the female clerical division, said, "Gloria, it had to be that way. We've been out a long time. Let someone else find this civilization."

The Grand Captain tapped with her pencil on the long, gleaming desk, an impatient gesture. But when she spoke, her voice was measured. "Regulation 492 gives me discre-tion to act as I see fit in a period varying between five and ten percent of the total length of the voyage to date, pro-vided the discretionary power is not employed beyond six months. I therefore decree that we remain six months longer in the Greater Magellanic Cloud. And now let us discuss ways and means of locating a planet of the Fifty Suns. Here are my ideas."

Coolly, she proceeded to give them.

III

Maltby was reading in his cabin aboard the Fifty Suns battleship *Atmion* when the alarm sounded. "All personnel to stations!"

There was no whine of sirens, so it was not a battle alert. He put down his book, slipped into his coat, and headed for the Astrogation and instrument room. Several officers, including the ship's executive astrogational officer, were already there when he arrived. They nodded to him rather curtly, but that was usual. He sat down at his desk and took out of his pocket the tool of his trade: a slide rule with a radio attachment that connected with the nearest—in this case the ship's—mechanical brain.

He was in the act of taking out pencils and paper when the ship moved under him. Simultaneously, a loud-speaker came on, and the unmistakable voice of Commanding Officer Vice-admiral Dreehan said:

"This message is going to officers only. As you know, slightly more than a week ago we were contacted by the Earth battleship *Star Cluster* and given an ultimatum, the time limit for which expired five hours ago. Up till now the various governments of our people have indicated that no further message has been forthcoming. Actually, a second ultimatum was received about three hours ago, but it contained an unexpected threat. It is believed that the public might be unduly alarmed if the nature of the threat was announced. The attitude of the governments will be that no second message was received. But here, for your private information, is the new ultimatum."

There was a pause, and then a deep, firm, resonant man's voice spoke: "Her excellency, the Right Honorable Gloria Cecily, Lady Laurr of Noble Laurr, Grand Captain of the

153

battleship *Star Cluster,* will now deliver her second message to the people of the Fifty Suns."

There was another pause. And then, instead of Grand Captain Laurr, Admiral Dreehan's voice came on again.

"I have been asked," he said, "to call your attention to this imposing list of titles. Apparently a woman of so-called noble birth is in command of the enemy ship. That a woman should be commander seems very democratic, indicating equality of the sexes. But how did she gain her appointment? Through her rank? Besides, the very existence of rank is some indication of the kind of totalitarian government that exists in the main galaxy."

Maltby could not agree to the analysis. Titles were words that had meanings according to usage. In the Fifty Suns, there had been totalitarian eras where the leaders called themselves "Chief Servant." There had been "Presidents" whose whim could mean death for individuals, "Secretaries" who controlled governments absolutely, immensely danger-ous individuals all, whose nominal rank covered a deadly reality. Furthermore, the desire for a verbal symbol of achievement permeated all human effort in every type of political system. Even as he spoke, "Admiral" Dreehan ex-ercised his rank. In listening to this private transcription of an ultimatum "Captain" Maltby was being given a special privilege of rank and position. The "head" of a business, the "owner" of property, the trained "expert"—each in its fashion was rank. Each gave the possessor emotional satis-faction similar to that obtainable from position of any de-gree. In the Fifty Suns it had become popular to despise kings and dictators of all history. This attitude, in failing to take account of the circumstances, was as childish as its op-posite: the inculcated worship of leaders. The Mixed Men, in their desperate situation, had reluctantly appointed a hereditary leader to avoid the bitter rivalry of ambitious men. Their plan had received a dangerous setback when the "heir" was captured. But the resulting struggle for pow-er had decided them to reaffirm his status. It seemed to Maltby, ruefully, that no man had ever felt so little like a hereditary ruler. Yet even as he shifted uneasily under the rank, he recognized how necessary it had been. And how great was the obligation upon him to act decisively in a crisis. His thought ended because her "excellency" was speaking.

Grand Captain the Right Honorable Gloria Cecily said:

"It is with regret that we who represent the Earth civilization recognize the recalcitrancy of the government of the Fifty Suns. We can say in the most solemn fashion that the people have been misled. The coming of Earth power into the Greater Magellanic Cloud will be of benefit to all individuals and groups of all planets. Earth has much to offer. Earth guarantees to the individual basic rights under law, guarantees to the group basic freedoms and economic prosperity, and requires all government to be elective by secret ballot.

"Earth does not permit a separate sovereign state *anywhere in the universe*.

"Such a separate military power could strike at the heart of the human-controlled galaxy and drop bombs on densely populated planets. That has happened. You may guess what we did to the governments who sponsored such a project. You cannot escape us. If by any chance we should fail now with our one ship to locate you, then within a few years ten thousand ships will be here searching. This is one thing we never delay on. From our point of view, it is safer to destroy an entire civilization than let it exist as a cancer in the greater culture from which it sprang.

"However, we do not think that we shall fail. Starting now, my great battleship, *Star Cluster*, will cruise on a definite course through the Greater Magellanic Cloud. It will take us several years to pass within five hundred light years of every sun in the system. As we move along, we shall direct cosmic-ray bombs at random toward the planets of most of the stars in any given area of space.

"Realizing that such a threat might make you afraid to trust yourselves to us, I have indicated why we adopt this admittedly merciless attitude. It is not yet too late to reveal yourselves. At any moment the government of any planet can broadcast its willingness to identify the location of the Fifty Suns. The first planet to do so will henceforth, and for all future time, be the capital of the Fifty Suns. The first individual or group who gives us a clue to the location of his or its planet will receive a gift of one billion platinum dollars, good anywhere in the main galaxy, or if you prefer, the equivalent sum in your own money.

"Have no fear. My ship can protect you against the organized might of the Fifty Suns military forces. And now, as an evidence of our determination, I shall have our chief astrogator broadcast the figures that will enable you to follow our course through the Cloud."

The message ended abruptly. Admiral Dreehan came on and said, "I shall presently give these figures to the Astrogation department, since it is our intention to follow the *Star Cluster* and observe the result of its announced program. However, I have been asked to call your attention to another implication to the broadcast which Lady Laurr has made to us. Her manner, tone, and wording suggest that she commands a very big ship." The admiral went on quickly: "Please do not imagine that we are jumping to any conclusions, but consider some of her statements. She says that the *Star Cluster* will 'direct' cosmic-ray bombs to most of the planets of the Cloud. Suppose, when reduced to common sense, she meant one bomb for every hundred planets. That would require several million bombs. But our own bomb factories can turn out only one cosmic-ray unit every four days. At a minimum, such a factory would need a square mile of floor space. Then again, she stated that her one ship can protect traitors against the Fifty Suns military forces. At the moment we have more than a hundred battleships in service in addition to four hundred cruisers and thousands of smaller craft. Let's consider also the original purpose of the *Star Cluster* in the Greater Magellanic Cloud. It was, by their own admission, a star-mapping expedition. Our own mapping ships are small obsolete models. It seems hard to believe that Earth would assign one of their greatest and most powerful ships to so routine a task." The admiral broke off. "I should like all officers to prepare for me their reactions to the foregoing statements. And now, that's all for most of you. I shall broadcast for Astrogation and Meteorology the figures supplied us by the *Star Cluster*."

It required just over five hours of sustained, careful work to orient the map furnished by the *Star Cluster* to the long-established star map system of the Fifty Suns. At that time it was estimated that the *Atmion* was about 1,400 light-years away from the Earth ship.

The distance was unimportant. They knew the location of all storms in the Greater Magellanic Cloud. And so they easily plotted an orbit that permitted a velocity of approximately half a light-year a minute.

The prolonged effort tired Maltby. As soon as his share of the task was finished, he retreated to his cabin and slept.

He woke to the sound of an alarm bell ringing. Quickly, he switched on a viewplate that connected with the bridge. The fact that a picture came on immediately indicated that officers were being permitted to watch events. He saw on the plate that it was focused at full magnification on a distant point of light. The light moved, and the plate kept adjusting, trying to hold it near center.

A voice said, "According to our automatic calculators, the *Star Cluster* is now approximately a third of a light-year away."

Maltby frowned at the explanation because it was not properly worded. The speaker meant that the two vessels were within each other's upper-resonance fields, a secondary phenomenon of subspace radio, and a kind of damped echo of the virtually unlimited lower-resonance range. It was impossible to tell how far away the Earth ship was, except that it could not be farther than a third of a light-year. It might be only a few hundred miles, though that was doubtful. There were radar devices for short-distance detection of objects in space.

The voice went on. "We have reduced our own speed to ten light-days a minute. Since we are following the course broadcast by the Earth ship and have not lost her, we can assume that we are matching her velocity."

That statement, also, was not exact. It was possible to approximate but impossible to *match* velocities with a ship traveling at more than light-speed. The error would show up as soon as the two ships lost touch with each other's upper-resonance fields. Even as he had thought, the light on the plate winked out.

Maltby waited, and finally the announcer said unhappily, "Please do not be alarmed. I have been told contact will probably be reestablished."

An hour went by, and the light did not reappear. Maltby had long since ceased paying more than sporadic attention

157

to the viewplate. His mind was on what Admiral Dreehan had said about the size of the *Star Cluster*.

He realized the commanding officer had stated the situation fairly. It was a problem laden with dangerous possibilities. It seemed impossible that any vessel could be as big as Grand Captain Laurr had implied. And therefore the Earth ship was putting on a bluff. At least a part of the proof would be in the number of bombs she set off.

On six successive days the *Atmion* entered the upper-resonance field of the Earth ship. Each time she maintained contact as long as possible; and then, having verified the enemy vessel's route, examined the planets of nearby suns. Only once did they find evidence of destruction. And the bomb must have been badly aimed, for it had hit an outer planet normally too cold and remote for its sun to support life.

It was not cold now but a seething hell of nuclear energy that had fired the rocky crust and penetrated to the metallic core itself. A miniature sun blazed there. The sight of it alarmed no one aboard the *Atmion*. The probability that one of a hundred bombs would strike an inhabited planet was mathematically so close to zero that the difference didn't count.

It was on the sixth day of the search when Maltby's viewplate clicked on; and the image of Vice-admiral Dreehan's face appeared on it. "Captain Maltby, will you report to my office?"

"Yes, sir."

Maltby went at once. The adjutant in charge nodded recognition and admitted him to Dreehan's cabin. Maltby found the commanding officer sitting in a chair, contemplating what looked like a radiogram. The older man laid the document face down and motioned Maltby to sit down in the chair across the desk.

"Captain, what is your status among the Mixed Men?"

So they had finally got around to that basic question.

Maltby did not feel alarmed. He stared at the officer and allowed an expression of puzzlement to creep over his face. Dreehan was a middle-aged Dellian with the fine physique and handsome appearance of his kind. Maltby said, "I couldn't tell you exactly how they regard me. Partly as a traitor, I think. Whenever they contact me—which I always report to my superiors—I urge the agent who talks to me to tell his superiors that I recommend a policy of conciliation and integrity."

Dreehan seemed to consider that, and then he said, "What do the Mixed Men think of this business?"

"I'm not sure. My contact is too vague."

"Still, you probably have some idea."

"As I understand it," said Maltby, "a minority group among them believes that Earth will locate the Fifty Suns sooner or later, so—they argue—advantage should be taken of the present position. The majority, which is tired of living in hiding, has definitely voted to go along with the rest of the Fifty Suns."

"By what percentage?"

"Just over four to one." Maltby spoke the lie without hesitation.

Dreehan hesitated; then he said, "Is there any possibility that the dissident minority will act unilaterally?"

Maltby said quickly, "They might want to, but they can't—so I've been assured."

"Why can't they?"

"They do not have a really skillful space meteorologist among them."

That was also a lie. The problem went deeper than any skill possessed by either group. The fact was that Hunston wanted to gain control of the Mixed Men by legal means. So long as he believed that he could do so, he would not take the law into his own hands—so Maltby's advisers had informed him. On that information, he now based his verbal web of falsehood and truth.

Dreehan seemed to be considering his words. He said finally, "The governments of the Fifty Suns are alarmed by the nature of the latest ultimatum—which you have heard—in that it offers such an ideal opportunity to the Mixed Men. They can betray us and gain advantages as great as might have been theirs had they won the war a generation ago."

There was nothing Maltby could say to that except repeat a variation of his earlier lie. "I think the four-to-one victory of those who prefer to stick with the Fifty Suns shows the trend."

159

Once more there was a pause. And Maltby wondered what was really behind the interview. Surely they couldn't be basing their hopes on reassurances from Captain Peter Maltby. Dreehan cleared his throat. "Captain, I've heard a great deal about the so-called double mind of the Mixed Men without ever getting a clear explanation of how it works and what it does. Will you enlighten me?"

"It's really quite unimportant." Maltby spoke his third lie quietly. "I think the fear of it during the war had a great deal to do with the ferocity with which the final battles were fought. You know what a normal brain is like—innumerable cells, each one separately connectable to those adjoining it. On that level, the brain of the Mixed Man is no different than yours. Go down another level, and you have in each cell of a Mixed Man a whole series of large, protein, *paired* molecules. Yours are not paired; his are."

"But what does that do?"

"The Mixed Man has the Dellian ability to resist the breaking down of his mind and the non-Dellian potentiality for creative work."

"That's all?"

"That's all that I know of, sir," lied Maltby.

"What about that devastating hypnosis they were supposed to have? There is no clear record of how that worked."

Maltby said, "I understand they used hypnotic *devices*, a very different thing. It caused a confused terror of the unknown."

Dreehan seemed to come to a decision. He picked up the radiogram and handed it to Maltby. "This came for you," he said. He added frankly, "If it's in code, we haven't been able to break it."

It was in code all right. Maltby saw that in the first glance. And this was what the Admiral had been leading up to.

The message read:
TO: Captain Peter Maltby,
 Aboard battleship *Atmion*

The government of the Mixed Men wishes to thank you for acting as mediator in the negotiations with the governments of the Fifty Suns. Please be assured that agreements will be lived up to fully and that the Mixed Men as a group are anxious to obtain the privileges that have been offered.

There was no signature. Which meant that the call for help had been sent by subspace radio and monitored directly by the *Atmion*.

He had to pretend of course that he didn't know that—until he could make up his mind what to do. He said in a puzzled tone, "I notice there's no signature. Was that left off on purpose?"

Vice-admiral Dreehan looked disappointed. "Your guess is as good as mine."

Maltby felt briefly sorry for the officer. No Dellian or non-Dellian would ever break the code of that message. Solving the secret of it depended on having two minds trained to associate. The training was so basic in the education of Mixed Men that Maltby had received a full quota before he was captured more than twenty years before.

The essential meat of the real message was that the minority group had announced its intention of contacting the *Star Cluster* and had begun a week-long campaign to gain support for the action. Their platform warned that only those who supported them would benefit from the betrayal.

He would have to go there in person. How? His eyes widened a little as he realized that he had only one available method of transportation: this ship. Abruptly, he knew that he had to do it. He began to tense his muscles in the Dellian fashion. He could feel the electric excitement of that stimulation. All in a moment his minds were strong enough.

He sensed the near presence of another mind. He waited till the sensation seemed to be a part of his own body; then he thought, *Blankness!* For a moment he held conscious thought away from his own brain. Finally, he stood up. Vice-admiral Dreehan stood up, also, in exactly the same way, with the same movements, as if his muscles were controlled by Maltby's brain. Which they were. He walked to the instrument board, touched a switch. "Give me the engine room," he said.

With Maltby's mind directing his voice and his actions, he gave the orders that set the *Atmion* on a course that would bring it presently to the hidden capital city of the Mixed Men.

IV

Grand Captain Laurr read the notice of "Nullification," sat for a few minutes with fists clenched, in anger. And then, controlling herself, called Captain Wayless. The officer's face stiffened as he saw who it was. "Captain," she said plaintively, "I have just read your document with its twenty-four signatures."

"It's legal, I believe," he said in a formal tone.

"Oh, I'm very sure of that," she retorted. She caught herself and went on: "Captain, why this desperate determination to go home immediately? Life is more than legality. We're engaged in a great adventure. Surely you have some of that feeling left in you."

"Madam," was the cool reply, "I have both admiration and affection for you. You have tremendous administrative ability, but you do tend to project your own ideas and are amazed and hurt when other people have notions different from your own. You are right so often that you lose sight of the fact that once in a while you may be wrong. That is why a big ship like this has thirty captains to advise you and, in an emergency, or actually at any time, overrule you according to prescribed regulations. Believe me, we all love you. But we know our duty to the rest of those aboard."

"But you're wrong. We can force this civilization out into the open." She hesitated, then, "Captain, won't you please go along with me just this once?"

It was a personal appeal, and she regretted almost immediately that she had made it. The request seemed to release his tension. He laughed, tried to hold himself, then laughed again.

"Madam, I beg your pardon," he said finally. "Please forgive me."

She was stiff. "What amused you?"

He was sober-faced again. "The phrase 'Just this once.' Lady Laurr, have you no recollection of ever having asked us to support some plan of yours before?"

"Perhaps a couple of times." She spoke with abrupt caution, remembering.

"I haven't figured it out," said Captain Wayless, "but just on a rough estimate I would say that you have either asked for our support on a personal basis or else have used your legal command status no less than a hundred times on this voyage to put over or enforce some idea of your own. Now, for once, the legality is being used against you. And you resent it bitterly."

"I'm not bitter. I'm—" She broke off. "Ohhhhh, I can see there's no use talking to you. For some reason or other you've decided that six months is all eternity."

"It's not a matter of time. It's a matter of the purpose. You believe without evidence that you can find fifty suns scattered among a hundred million. A big ship just does not take a one-in-two-million chance of that kind. If you can't see that, then for once we have to overrule you regardless of our personal affection for you."

The Grand Captain hesitated. The argument was going against her. She saw the need for a more careful presentation of her reasons. She said slowly, "Captain, this is not a mechanical problem. If we were depending on chance alone, then your attitude would be correct. Our hope must be based on psychology."

Captain Wayless said quietly, "Those of us who signed the 'Nullification' did not do so lightly. We discussed the psychological aspect."

"And on what did you base your rejection of it? Ignorance?"

It was a sharp remark, and she saw that he was irritated. He said formally, "Madam, we have on occasion noted with misgivings your tendency to rely almost exclusively on the advice offered you by Lieutenant Neslor. These meetings you have with her are always private. What is said in them is never brought into the open, except that suddenly you make a move based on what she has told you."

The picture startled her a little. She said defensively, "I confess I hadn't thought of it that way. I merely went to the legally appointed chief psychologist aboard this ship."

Captain Wayless went on. "If Lieutenant Neslor's advice is so valuable, then she should be raised to captain's rank and permitted to air her views before the other captains."

He shrugged, and he must almost have read her thought. Because, before she could utter the words, he said, "And please don't say that you will immediately make the appointment. It takes a month for such a promotion to be put through even if no one objects; and the new captain then sits silent for two months learning the procedure at a council meeting."

Lady Laurr said grimly, "You won't permit such a three-month delay?"

"No."

"You won't consider by-passing ordinary procedure in making such an appointment?"

"In an emergency, yes. But this is merely a notion of yours for finding a lost civilization—which will be searched for and found eventually by an expedition dispatched for that purpose."

"Then you insist on 'Nullification'?"

"Yes."

"Very well. I shall order a plebiscite for two weeks from today. If it goes against me, and if nothing else turns up, we start for home."

With a gesture, she broke the connection.

She thought of herself consciously as engaged in warfare on two levels. On the one level, there was the struggle against Captain Wayless and the four-fifths majority that had enabled him to force a plebiscite. On the other there was the fight she was waging to force the Fifty Suns people out into the open. On both levels, she had just begun to fight. She called "Communication." Captain Gorson answered. She said, "Are we still in touch with the Fifty Suns ship that is observing us?"

"No. I reported to you when we lost contact. It has not yet been reestablished." He volunteered, "They'll probably pick us up again tomorrow when we broadcast our position at that time."

"Advise me."

"Of course."

She broke the connection and called "Weapons." A subordinate answered, but she waited patiently till the captain in charge was called. Then:

"How many bombs have you dropped?"

"Seven altogether."

"All dropped at random?"

"It's the simplest method, madam. Probability protects us from hitting a planet capable of supporting life."

She nodded but sat frowning anxiously. She said, finally, feeling the need to restate the situation, "Intellectually, I agree with that. Emotionally—" She broke off. "A single mistake, Captain, and you and I would be put on trial for our lives if it were ever found out."

He was grim. "I am familiar with that law, your excellency. It is one of the hazards of being in charge of 'Weapons.'" He hesitated, then, "My feeling is that you made a very dangerous threat—dangerous to us, that is. People should not be subjected to such pressures."

She said curtly, "That's my responsibility!" And broke the connection.

She stood up then and paced the floor. Two weeks! It seemed impossible that anything could happen before then. In two weeks, as she had planned it, the psychological pressure on the Dellians and non-Dellians would barely have begun.

Thought of them reminded her. She walked swiftly to the matter transmitter, made the adjustments—and stepped through to the centrally located library, just over a third of a mile from her quarters.

She found herself in the private office of the chief librarian, who was sitting at her desk, writing. The Grand Captain began instantly. "Jane, have you got that information on the Dellian riots of—"

The librarian started, half-rose from her chair, then sat down again. She sighed. "Gloria, you'll be the death of me. Can't you even say hello before you start in?"

The Grand Captain felt contrite. "I'm sorry. I was intent. But have you—"

"Yes, I have. If you'd waited another ten minutes, it would have been sent up to you in an orderly fashion. Have you had dinner yet?"

"Dinner! No, of course not."

"I love the way you say that. And, knowing you, I know exactly what you mean. Well, you're coming to dinner with me. And there'll be no discussion of Dellians or non-Dellians until after we've eaten."

"It's impossible, Jane. I just can't give the time right now—"

The older woman had climbed to her feet. Now, she came around the desk and took Lady Laurr firmly by the arm. "Oh, you can't. Then just consider this. You will not receive any information from me until you've had dinner. And go right ahead and invoke your laws and regulations, and see if I care. Come along now."

For a second she resisted. Then she thought wearily: *It's this damned human factor. It's too hard to make people realize!* That tension ended, also, and she had a sudden picture of herself, grim and intent, as if the fate of the universe rested on her shoulders. Slowly, she relaxed. She said, "Thank you, Jane. I'd love to have a glass of wine and some dinner."

But she did not forget that she was right, that, though she might relax for an hour, the reality remained. The Fifty Suns had to be found now for a reason that was only gradually maturing in her brain in all its deadly potentialities.

After dinner, with soft music playing in the background, they discussed the Fifty Suns civilization. The historical outline, as given by the librarian, was remarkably simple and straightforward.

Some fifteen thousand years before, Joseph M. Dell had developed an early variation of the matter transmitter. The machine required mechanical synthesis of certain types of tissue, particularly of the endocrine glands, that could not be properly scanned. Since a human being could step in at one end and emerge an instant later a thousand miles or more—or less—away, it was not immediately noticed that extremely subtle changes were taking place in the individuals who used the method of teleportation.

It was not that anything was missing, though Dellians were always afterward slow at creative work. But in some respects something seemed to have been added.

The Dellian proved to be less subject to nervous strain. His physical strength far exceeded anything ever dreamed of by human beings. He could build himself up to superhuman effort by a curious process of internal stepping up of muscular tension.

Naturally—the librarian was ironic when she came to

that part—they were called robots by the more alarmed of human beings. The name did not disturb the Dellians, but it excited humans to a height of hatred that was not immediately suspected by the authorities.

There was a period when mobs raged along the streets lynching Dellians. Human friends of the Dellians persuaded the government to let them migrate. Until now, no one had ever known where they had gone to.

The Right Honorable Gloria Cecily sat thoughtful for a while after the account was completed. She said finally, "You haven't been really helpful. I knew all that, except for a couple of minor details."

She was aware of the older woman studying her with shrewd blue eyes. "Gloria, what are you after? When you talk like that, you're usually trying to prove a theory of your own."

The remark hit home. The Grand Captain saw that it might be dangerous for her to admit such a thing. People who tried to force facts to fit their own private theories were unscientific. She had frequently been very sharp with officers who uttered vague opinions. She said slowly, "I simply want all the information we can get. It's obvious that when a mutation like the Dellian is off somewhere for a hundred and fifty centuries all the possible eventualities will have taken place. My attitude is, we can't afford to miss a single point that is available."

The librarian nodded. Watching her, Lady Laurr decided that the explanation had proved satisfactory and that the momentary insight had faded from the forefront of the other's mind.

She stood up. She couldn't take the chance of any further revelations. The second one might not be so easy to dismiss. She said good night casually and returned to her quarters. After a few minutes of thought, she called "Biology," and asked as her first question, "Doctor, I have previously sent you information on the Dellian and non-Dellian peoples of the Fifty Suns. In your opinion, would it be possible for a Dellian and non-Dellian—married to each other—to have children?"

The biologist was a slow-thinking man who drawled when he spoke. "History says no," he said.

"What do you say?"

"I could do it."

"That," said Grand Captain Laurr triumphantly, "is what I wanted to hear."

The stimulation the information brought her did not fade until she crept into bed hours later. She turned out the light, then, and lay for a while staring out into space.

The great night was slightly changed. The points of light were differently arranged, but without magnification she had no visual evidence that she was actually in the Greater Magellanic Cloud. Not more than a hundred individual stars showed as separate units. Here and there was a fuzziness of light that indicated the presence of hundreds of thousands of stars, perhaps millions.

On impulse, she reached toward the vision control and turned the magnification to full.

Splendor.

A billion stars blazed at her. She saw the near brillance of innumerable stars in the Cloud and the vast spiral wheel of the main galaxy, impregnated now with more light-points than could ever be counted. And all that she could see was a mere speck in the cosmic scheme of things. Where had it come from? Tens of thousands of generations of human beings had lived and died, and there was still not even the beginning of a satisfactory answer.

She reduced magnification to zero and brought the universe back to the level of her own senses. Wide-eyed, she thought, "Suppose they did produce a cross-breed of the Dellian and non-Dellian? How could that affect me in two weeks?"

She couldn't imagine. She slept restlessly.

Morning . . . As she ate her lean breakfast, it struck her that only thirteen days remained. The impact of that hit her suddenly. She got up from the table, gloomily conscious that she was living in a dream world. Unless she took positive action, the entire enterprise upon which she had launched the great ship would collapse. She headed decisively for the control bridge and called Communications. "Captain," she said to the officer who answered, "are we in upper-resonance contact with the Fifty Suns ship that is trailing us?"

"No, madam."

That was disappointing. Now that she had made up her

mind, any delay was irritating. She hesitated, finally sighed her acceptance of the reality, and said, "The moment contact is made, communicate to Weapons."

"Very well, madam."

She broke connection and called Weapons. The proud-faced officer commanding that department swallowed as she explained her purpose. He protested finally. "But, madam, this would reveal our greatest weapon. Suppose—"

"Suppose nothing!" Her fury was instant. "At this stage we have nothing to lose. We have failed to lure the Fifty Suns fleet. I order you to capture that one vessel. All the Navigation officers aboard will probably be ordered to commit suicide, but we'll get around that."

The officer frowned thoughtfully, then nodded. "The danger is that someone outside the field will detect it and analyze it. But if you feel we should take that risk—"

The Right Honorable Gloria turned presently to other tasks, but a part of her mind never quite let go of the command she had given. She grew restless finally when no further call came, and again contacted Communications. But there was nothing. The Fifty Suns ship was not in range.

A day went by, then another. And still no contact.

By the fourth day, the Grand Captain of the *Star Cluster* was a very difficult person to get along with. And that day also went by without incident.

V

"Planet below!" said Vice-admiral Dreehan.

Maltby, who had been cat-napping, woke with a start, climbed to his feet, and went to the controls.

Under his direction, the ship moved rapidly from ten thousand miles above the surface to a thousand, and then to less than a hundred miles. Through magnification, he examined the terrain; and presently, though he had never seen it before, his memory brought up photographic maps he had been shown in the past.

Rapidly, now, the *Atmion* headed toward the largest of the cave entrances that led down to the hidden capital of the Mixed Men. As a final precaution, he checked once more to make sure that junior officers were not able to watch what was happening in their viewplates—all fourteen senior key men were under his control—and then boldly he nosed the ship into the opening.

He watched tensely. He had radioed the leaders who supported him that he was coming. They had called back to say that all would be in readiness. But it was possible for a slip-up to occur. And here at the entrance a ship would be at the mercy of ground defenses.

The darkness of the cave closed around them. He sat with fingers on the searchlight switch, watching the night ahead. Suddenly, a light flickered far below. Maltby waited to make sure that it would not go out and then flicked the switch.

Instantly, the searchlights glared, lighting up the cave from ceiling to floor and into the distance ahead. The ship cruised forward and gradually downward. An hour went by; and still there was no indication that the end of the journey was near.

The cave curved and twisted, downward and sideways and upward. Several times he had the feeling that they were going back the way they had come. He could have kept track on an automatic graph, but he had been asked even before the *Atmion* neared the planet not to do so. It was said that no living person knew exactly where under the planet's crust the capital was located. Other Mixed Men cities on still other planets were hidden in the same way.

Twelve hours passed. Twice Maltby had turned the control over to the Vice-admiral while he slept. Now, he was in charge while the officer dozed peacefully on the cot in the corner.

Thirty hours! Physically worn out and amazed, Maltby wakened Dreehan and lay down. He had scarcely closed his eyes when the officer said:

"Buildings ahead, Captain. Lights."

Maltby made a leap for the controls and a few minutes later was guiding the ship over a city of about eighty thousand population. He had been told that no vessel of its size had ever been in the caves; and therefore at this moment it would be the object of attention by all individuals and groups. He switched on ordinary radio and turned the dial till he heard a voice. He heard: ". . . and Peter Maltby, our hereditary leader, has temporarily taken over the battleship *Atmion* in order that he might personally reason with those who—"

Maltby clicked it off. The people were learning that he was here. In the plate, he searched the city below for Hunston's headquarters. He recognized the building from the description he had been radioed and stopped the *Atmion* directly over it.

He focused an energy screen on the center of the street a block away. Then, swiftly, he laid down other screens till the area was completely blocked off. People could enter the screen area without noticing that they were coming into a trap, but they could not leave it. Invisible from the outside, the screen had a purplish tint when seen from inside. It gave anyone who touched it from the inner section a powerful electric shock.

Since Hunston lived at his headquarters, it seemed likely that he was now unable to escape. Maltby did not delude himself that the action would be decisive. This was a struggle for political control, that might be influenced by force but would not be resolved on that basis alone. In that struggle his very method of arrival had given his enemies a powerful argument against him. "Look," they would undoubtedly say, "one Mixed Man was able to take over a battleship—proof of our superiority." That was heady stuff for people whose ambition had been starved for a quarter of a century.

In the viewplate he saw that small craft were approaching. He contacted them by radio, identified those aboard as leaders who supported him, and presently watched as his officer-controls personally admitted them to the airlock. Minutes later he was shaking hands with men he had never before seen in person.

Tactical and strategical discussions began almost immediately. Several men who came aboard felt that Hunston should be executed. A majority believed that he should be imprisoned. Maltby listened uneasily to both groups, conscious that in a sense the men on the scene were the best judges. On the other hand, their very closeness to the danger had made them tense. It was even possible that he, who had watched this scene from afar, might have a more detached and therefore sounder attitude. That was a guess only, and he did not give too much weight to it. Nevertheless, he had begun to regard himself as being in the role of an arbiter when, abruptly, both groups began to question him.

"Can we be sure that the Fifty Suns will remain firm in their refusal to establish contact with the Earth ship?"

"Was there any sign of weakening from what you saw and heard?"

"Why was the second ultimatum withheld from the people?"

"Is the battleship *Atmion* the only ship assigned to follow the *Star Cluster?*"

"Is there perhaps some secret purpose behind such a following move?"

"What would our position be if suddenly the Fifty Suns surrendered their location?"

For a little while, Maltby felt overwhelmed. And then, as he saw that the questions followed a pattern, and that behind them was a false implication, he held up his hand and said, "Gentlemen, you seem to be laboring under the theory that if the other governments should change their minds, we might still rush in and gain an advantage. This is not so. Our position is that we stand solidly with the

Fifty Suns whatever their decision. We act as one with the group. We do not maneuver for special advantage other than within the frame of the offer that has been made to us." He finished in a more personal, less severe tone. "I can see you have all been under immense pressure. Believe me, I appreciate your position as a group and as individuals. But we've got to maintain our integrity. We cannot be opportunistic in this crisis."

The men looked at each other. Some, particularly the younger men, seemed unhappy, as if they were being asked to swallow a bitter pill. But in the end they all agreed to support the plan for the time being.

Then came the crucial question. "What about Hunston?"

Maltby said coolly, "I'd like to talk to him."

Collings, the oldest personal friend of Maltby's father, studied Maltby's face for several seconds and then walked into the radio room. He was pale when he came back. "He refuses to come up here. He says if you want to see him, you can come down. Peter, this is outrageous."

"Tell him," said Maltby steadily, "that I'll be right down."

He smiled at their dour faces. "Gentlemen," he said in a ringing tone, "this man is playing into our hands. Broadcast that I'm going down for the sake of amity in a great crisis. Don't overdo it, but put just a hint of doubt into your announcement, indicating that possibly violence will be done me."

He finished matter-of-factly. "Obviously, nothing will happen, with this ship floating here in a dominant position. However, if I'm not back in an hour and a half, try to contact me. Then, step by step, beginning with threats, reach the point where you start shooting."

Despite his confidence he had a curious feeling of emptiness and aloneness as his lifeboat settled down on the roof of Hunston's headquarters.

Hunston was a tall, sardonic-looking man in his middle thirties. As Maltby entered his private office, he stood up, came forward, and shook hands. He said in a quiet, pleasant voice, "I wanted to get you away from those wet hens who rule the roost down here. No *lese majesty* was intended. I want to talk to you. I think I can convince you."

He made the attempt in a low, cultured, but very alive voice. His arguments were the stale arguments of the basic superiority of the Mixed Men. He obviously believed his own premises, and in the end Maltby could not escape the conviction that the man's main fault was lack of general and specific information about the world outside. He had lived too long in this narrow environment of the Mixed Men cities, spent too many years talking and thinking without reference to larger realities. Despite his brilliance, Hunston was provincially minded.

The rebel leader completed his monologue and asked a question. "Do you believe that the Fifty Suns will be able to remain hidden from Earth civilization?"

"No," said Maltby truthfully. "I believe eventual discovery is inevitable."

"Yet you support their deluded attempt to remain secret?"

"I support unity in dealing with the situation. I believe it is wise to be cautious in accepting contact. It is even possible that we could hold off discovery for a hundred years, perhaps longer."

Hunston was silent. There was a scowl on his handsome face. "I can see," he said at last, "that we hold opposite views."

Watching the man, Maltby said slowly, "Perhaps our long-run intentions are the same. Perhaps we merely have different plans for arriving at the same goal."

Hunston's face lighted; his eyes widened slightly. He said eagerly, "Your excellency, if I could believe that." He broke off, his eyes narrowing abruptly. "I'd like to hear your opinion of the future role of the Mixed Men in civilization."

"Given the opportunity, using legal methods," said Maltby quietly, "they will inevitably gravitate toward positions of top leadership. Without taking unfair advantage of their ability to control others mentally, they will first dominate the Fifty Suns and then the main galaxy. If at any time in their rise to power they use force, they will be destroyed to the last man, woman, and child."

Hunston's eyes were bright. "And how long do you think it will take?" he asked.

"It can begin in your lifetime and mine. It will require at least a thousand years, depending on how rapidly Dellians and human beings intermarry—as of now, children are forbidden in such marriages, as you know—"

Hunston nodded scowling; then he said: "I have been misinformed about your attitude. You are one of us."

"No!" Maltby spoke firmly. "Please do not confuse a long-run with a short-term attitude. It's the difference in this case between life and death. Even to mention that we expect in the end to gain domination would alarm people who have now been prepared by their governments to be cautiously friendly. If we show our unity regarding this issue, we can make a beginning. If we are opportunistic, then this little race of supermen of which you and I are members will sooner or later be destroyed."

Hunston was on his feet. "Your excellency, I'll accept that. I'll go along with you. We'll await developments."

It was an unexpected victory for him who had come prepared to use force. Despite his belief, however, that Hunston was sincere, he had no intention of merely taking the other's word. The man might change his mind as soon as the threat of the *Atmion* was removed. He said so, frankly, and finished: "Under the circumstances, I'll have to ask you to submit to a six-month term of imprisonment at some point where you cannot be in touch with your supporters. It will be merely a form of house arrest. You can take your wife. You will receive every courtesy and be freed immediately if contact is established in the meantime between the Earth ship and the Fifty Suns. Your position will be that of hostage rather than prisoner. I'll give you twenty-four hours to think it over."

No attempt was made to stop him as he returned to his lifeboat, and so back to the warship.

Hunston surrendered himself at the end of the twenty-four-hour period. He specified one condition: the terms of his house arrest must be broadcast.

And so the Fifty Suns were safe from immediate discovery, it being obvious that one ship could not without aid find even one planet of so well hidden a civilization. Maltby was convinced of it. There remained the problem of the inevitable discovery when other ships came from the main galaxy a few years hence. Curiously, now that the main danger was over, that began to worry him. As he guided the Fifty Suns battleship *Atmion* back on its original course, Maltby considered just what he might do to ensure further the safety of the people of the Greater Magellanic Cloud.

Somebody, it seemed to him, ought to find out just how great the danger was. The mere notion of how that would have to be done made him shaky; and yet with each passing hour he found himself becoming more determined and more convinced that he with his good will was the one person best suited to do the job.

He was still considering how he might let his ship be captured when the alarms began to sound.

"*Lady Laurr, we have established upper-resonance contact with a vessel of this system.*"

"*Seize it!*"

VI

Just how it was done, Maltby had no clear idea. In the early stages of the capture, he was too willing to be caught. By the time tractor beams gripped the *Atmion* it was a little late to analyze how the invader ship had maneuvered his own craft into the tractor-beam field.

Something happened, a physical sensation of being sucked into a vortex, a perceived tension and contortion of his own body, as if the basic matter of which he was composed was being subjected to strain. Whatever it was ended abruptly as the tractors took hold, and the Fifty Suns battleship was drawn toward the remote darkness where the other ship lay to, still hidden by distance.

Anxiously, Maltby watched the measuring instruments that might give him some estimate of the other vessel's size. As the minutes sped by, he began to realize it was improbable he would actually see the enemy machine. In that vast night even nearby suns were dim points of light. The characteristics of any body out here could only be determined over a period of time. Anything as small as a ship was like a dust mote lost in inconceivable darkness.

His doubts were realized. When the *Atmion* was still several light-minutes from its captor, a sharp, tortuous pain twisted his muscles. He had time to guess: paralyzer ray. And then he was writhing on the floor of the control room, with darkness closing over him.

He woke up, tense, wary, convinced that he had to seize control of the situation, whatever it might be. He guessed that there would be methods for controlling his mind and forcing it to give information. He must even assume that his own powerful double brain could be overcome, once its potentialities were suspected.

He opened his eyes ever so slightly by relaxing the muscles of the eyelids. It was as if he had given a signal. From somewhere nearby a man said in an odd but understandable English:

"All right, ease her through the lock."

Maltby closed his eyes, but not before he had recognized that he was still inside the *Atmion*. And that apparently the process of taking the Fifty Suns battleship into the captor machine was just under way. The fact that he was still lying where he had fallen in the control room seemed to indicate that the officers and crew of the *Atmion* had not yet been questioned.

A wave of excitement swept through him. Was it going to be as simple as that? Was it possible that all he need do was probe cautiously with his two minds—and take control of any human being he contacted? And thus take control of the boarding crew? Was all that going to be possible?

It was. It happened.

Maltby was herded with the others along a corridor that stretched into the distance ahead. Armed crew members of the Earth ship—both men and women—walked ahead and behind the long line of captives.

It was an illusion. The real prisoners were the officers in charge of the prisoners. At the proper moment, the commander—a sturdy young man of forty or so—quietly ordered the main body of captives to continue along the corridor. But Maltby and the other officers from Astrogation and Meteorology were taken down a side corridor and into a large apartment with half a dozen bedrooms.

The Earth officer said matter-of-factly, "You'll be all right here. We'll bring proper uniforms, and you can move around the ship whenever you wish—provided you don't talk to our people too much. We've got all kinds of dialects aboard but none quite like yours. We don't want you to be noticed, so watch yourselves!"

Maltby was not worried. His problem, as he saw it, was to familiarize himself with the ship and its procedures. It was already obvious that it was a huge vessel and that there were more people aboard than one man could ever control directly. He suspected that there also were traps for the unwary intruder. But that was something that had to be risked. Once he had a general picture of the ship and its departments, he would quickly explore the unknown dangers.

When the "captors" had gone, he joined the other Astrogation men in a raid on the kitchen. As he had half anticipated,

179

there were many similarities in food. The Dellian and non-
Dellian humanoids had brought domesticated animals with
them millennia ago. And now here in these deep freezers
were steer steaks, pork and lamb chops, roasts and an enormous variety of Earth-origin fowl, each in its airtight transparent wrapper.

The men ate to satiation, and Maltby discussed in serious
vein with them the mystery of why they were being treated
as they were. He was acutely conscious of the fact that he
had done a dangerous thing. There were sharp minds present; and if one of them ever made a connection between
what had happened and the fear the Fifty Suns people had
of the Mixed Men, his report might well frighten his superiors more than the Earth ship. He was relieved when
the officer he controlled came back with a supply of uniforms.

The problem of control in front of Fifty Suns men was
a delicate one. It involved the "slave" believing that he was
doing what he was for a rational reason. The reason the
man had accepted was that he was acting under orders to
win the good will of the most valuable officers on the captured ship. He had the impression, moreover, that it would
be unwise to communicate this information directly to his
charges, and that he must not discuss it with brother officers of the ship.

As a result he was quite prepared to supply the indoctrina-
tion that would enable Maltby and the others to move in a
limited fashion about the *Star Cluster*. He was not prepared
to give them too much data about the ship itself. So long
as the others were present, Maltby accepted the limitation. But it was he who accompanied the officer when the
latter, feeling his job done, finally departed. To Maltby's
chagrin, the man proved invulnerable to mind control when
it came to information about the ship. He was willing, but
he *couldn't* impart that kind of data. Something—some sup-
pressor on him, perhaps hypnotic in nature—prevented. It
seemed clear, finally, that Maltby would have to learn what
he wanted to know from higher officers who had freedom
of choice. Lower-rank officers obviously did not, and the
method used to protect them was one that he couldn't take
the time to analyze and overcome.

He guessed that the ship's authorities would by now be

discovering that *Atmion*'s astrogators and meteorologists were missing. Somebody would be concerned about that in the determined and grim fashion of the military mind. If only he could get a chance to talk to the woman who was commander-in-chief of the Earth ship . . . But that in itself would make other steps essential. Escape?

Though it was important that he waste no time, it nevertheless required two hours more to control the officers who had charge of the captured Fifty Suns people and of the *Atmion*—to control them in such a way that, at a given signal, they would coordinate their actions and arrange an escape. In each case it was necessary to produce an actual or hallucinatory command from a superior officer in order to obtain the automatic acquiescence of the individual. As a precaution Maltby also provided the explanation that the *Atmion* was to be released as a friendly gesture to the Fifty Suns government.

That done, he successfully conveyed to a top officer that the Grand Captain insisted on seeing him. Just how it would all work out, Maltby had only the vaguest idea.

Lieutenant Neslor came onto the bridge and deposited her gaunt body in a chair. She sighed. "Something is wrong," she said.

The Grand Captain turned from what she had been doing at the control board and studied the older woman thoughtfully. She shrugged finally with a hint of anger in her manner and said in irritation, "Surely some of these Fifty Suns people know where their planets are."

The psychologist shook her head. "We have found no Astrogation officers aboard. The other prisoners were as surprised at that as I was."

Lady Laurr frowned. "I don't think I understand." She spoke slowly.

"There are five of them," said Lieutenant Neslor. "All were seen a few minutes before we captured the *Atmion*. Now, they're missing."

The younger woman said quickly, "Search the ship! Sound a general attention!" She half turned back to the great instrument board and then stopped herself. Thoughtfully, she faced the psychologist. "I see you don't consider that is the method."

"We've already had one experience with a Dellian," was the reply.

The Lady Gloria shuddered slightly. The memory of Gisser Watcher, the man who had been captured on the meteorite station, was still not completely resolved within her. She said finally, "What do you suggest?"

"Wait! They must have had a plan, whatever method they used to escape our energy control. I'd like to see where they try to go, what they want to find out."

"I see." The Grand Captain made no comment. She seemed to be gazing far away.

"Naturally," said Lieutenant Neslor, "you'll have to be protected. I'll make that my personal task."

Lady Laurr shrugged. "I really can't imagine how a newcomer aboard this ship could ever hope to find my apartment. If I should ever forget the method, I wouldn't care to have to figure out how to get back here." She broke off. "Is that all you have to suggest? Just wait and see what happens?"

"That's all."

The young woman shook her head. "That's not enough for me, my dear. I'm assuming that my earlier commands about precautions have been taken and are still in force." She turned abruptly to the control board. A moment later a face came on the plate. "Ah, Captain," said Gloria, "what are your police doing right now?"

"Searching and guarding," was the reply.

"Any success?"

"The ship is completely guarded against accidental explosions. All bombs are accounted for, with remote-control observers watching key entrances. No surprise is possible."

"Good," said Grand Captain Laurr. "Carry on." She broke the connection and yawned. "I guess it's bedtime. I'll be seeing you, my dear."

Lieutenant Neslor stood up. "I feel fairly sure that you can sleep safely."

She went out. The younger woman spent half an hour dictating memos to various departments, adjusting for each one the time at which it should be communicated. Presently, she undressed and went to bed. She was asleep almost at once.

She awakened with an odd sense of dissatisfaction. Except for the ever so faint glow from the instrument board, the bridge was in darkness, but after a moment she thought in amazement, "There's someone in the room."

She lay very still, savoring the menace, and remembering what Lieutenant Neslor had said. It seemed incredible that anyone unfamiliar with this monstrously large vessel should have located her so quickly. Her eyes were becoming accustomed to the darkness now, and in that dimness she was able to make out the silhouette of a man standing a few feet from her bed.

He must have been waiting for her to discover him. He must have been aware, somehow, that she was awake, for he said, "Don't turn on the light. And be very careful."

His voice was soft, almost gentle; yet it convinced her that the speaker was an extremely dangerous man. His command held her in the bed and kept her hand where it was on the sheet, unmoving. It even brought the first anguish of fear, the realization that before any help could reach her she might die. She could only hope that Lieutenant Neslor was awake and watching.

The intruder spoke again: "Nothing will happen to you if you do exactly as I say."

"*Who are you?*" Her tone conveyed her will to know.

Maltby did not answer. He had located a chair now, and he settled himself into it, but he was not happy with his situation. There were too many mechanical devices aboard a battleship for him to feel any sense of security in what he was doing. He could be defeated, even destroyed, without warning. He could imagine that, even now, the scene was under observation from some remote source beyond his power to control. He said slowly, "Madam, nothing will happen to you if you yourself make no overt moves. I'm here with the hope of having a few questions answered. To ease your mind, I am one of the astrogators of the Fifty Suns ship, *Atmion*. I won't go into the details of how we escaped your net, but I'm here talking to you this way because of your propaganda. You were right in thinking that there are differences of opinion among the people of the Fifty Suns. Some feel that we should accept your assurances. Others are afraid. Naturally, the fearful ones being in the majority have won. It always seems safer to wait and hope."

He paused and went back over his words with his

mind's ear; and though he could have worded them better—so it seemed to him—they sounded right in essence. If the people of this ship could ever be persuaded to believe anything he might say at this moment, it would be that he and others like him were still undecided. Maltby continued in the same careful, unhurried vein. "I represent a group that occupies a unique position in this affair. Only the astrogators and meteorologists on the various planets and ships are able to communicate the position of inhabited worlds. There are probably tens of thousands of would-be traitors who would betray their people in a moment for personal gain, but they are not among the trained and disciplined personnel of the government or the forces. I'm sure you will understand well what that means." He paused again to give her time to understand it.

The woman had relaxed gradually as Maltby talked. His words sounded rational, his intentions strange but not unbelievable. What bothered her was almost tiny by comparison: How had he found his way to her apartment? Anyone less familiar than she with the intricacies of the ship's operation might have accepted the reality of his presence and let it go at that. But she knew the laws of chance that were involved. It was as if he had come into a strange city of thirty thousand inhabitants and—without previous knowledge—walked straight to the home of the person he wanted to see. She shook her head ever so slightly, rejecting the explanation. She waited, nevertheless, for him to continue. His words had already reassured her as to her safety, and every moment that passed would make it more certain that Lieutenant Neslor was on the job. She might even learn something.

Maltby said, "We have to have some information. The decision you are trying to force upon us is one that we should all like to postpone. For us, it would be so much simpler if you would return to the main galaxy and send other ships back here at some later date. Then there would be time to adjust to the inevitable, and no one need be in the unenviable position of having to think of betraying his people."

Gloria nodded in the darkness. This she could understand. She said, "What questions do you want answered?"

"How long have you been in the Greater Magellanic Cloud?"

"Ten years."

Maltby went on. "How much longer do you plan to stay?"

"That information is not available," said the Grand Captain, her voice steady. It struck her that the statement was true even so far as she herself was concerned. The plebiscite would not take place for two days.

Maltby said, "I strongly advise that you answer my questions."

"What will happen if I don't?"

As she spoke, her hand, which she had moved carefully toward a small instrument board at the edge of her bed, attained its goal. Triumphantly, she pressed one of the buttons. She relaxed instantly. Out of the darkness Maltby said, "I decided to let you do that. I hope it makes you feel more secure."

His calmness disconcerted her, but she wondered if he understood clearly what she had done. Coolly, she explained that she had activated a bank of what was known as sensitive lights. From this moment on they would watch him with their numerous electronic eyes. Any attempt on his part to use an energy weapon would be met by counteracting forces. It also prevented her from using a weapon, but it seemed unwise to mention that.

Maltby said, "I have no intention of using an energy weapon. But I'd like you to answer more questions."

"I might." She spoke mildly, but she was beginning to be irritated with Lieutenant Neslor. Surely some action was now indicated.

Maltby said, "How big a ship is this?"

"It's fifteen hundred feet long and carries a complement of three thousand officers and lower ranks."

"That's pretty big," said Maltby. He was impressed and wondered how much she was exaggerating.

The Grand Captain made no comment. The real size was ten times what she had stated. But it wasn't size that counted so much as the quality of what was inside. She felt fairly sure that this interrogator had not even begun to understand how tremendous was the defensive and offensive potential of the vast ship she commanded. Only a few higher officers understood the nature of some of the forces

185

that could be brought into play. At the moment those officers were supposed to be under constant surveillance by remote-control observers.

Maltby said, "I'm puzzled as to just how we were captured. Could you explain that to me?"

So he had finally came around to that. Lady Laurr raised her voice. "Lieutenant Neslor."

"Yes, noble lady." The reply came promptly from somewhere in the darkness.

"Don't you think this comedy has gone on long enough?"

"I do indeed. Shall I kill him?"

"No. I want *him* to answer some questions."

Maltby took control of her mind as he walked hurriedly to the transmitter. Behind him—

"Don't fire!" said Gloria in an intense voice. "Let him go!"

Even afterward she did not seriously question that command or the impulse that had driven her to say it. Her explanation to herself—later—was that since the intruder had not threatened her and since he was one of the much-wanted astrogators, to destroy him in order to prevent his escaping to some other part of the ship would be an irrational act.

As a result Maltby left the bridge safely and was able to give the signal that freed the *Atmion*. As the Fifty Suns vessel fled into the distance, the officers of the Earth ship —acting on the final cue from him—began to forget their share in the escape.

Mentally, that was as far as Maltby had gotten. To enter the enemy vessel and to get away again—it had seemed a big enough venture in itself. What he had learned was not altogether satisfactory, but he did know they were dealing with a very large vessel. It was a vessel that would have to be careful in its dealings with a fleet, but he did not doubt that it had weapons capable of destroying several Fifty Suns battleships at the same time.

What bothered him was, how would the officers and crew of the *Atmion*, and the Fifty Suns people in general, react to the incident? That seemed too complex for any one man to calculate. And as for what would happen aboard the *Star Cluster*—that was even more difficult to forecast.

All the reaction did not show immediately. Maltby was

aware that Admiral Dreehan made a report to the Fifty Suns government. But for two days nothing occurred.

On the third day the *Star Cluster's* daily broadcast of its course showed that it had drastically altered its direction. The reason for the change was obscure.

On the fourth day, Maltby's viewplate lighted with the image of Vice-admiral Dreehan. The commanding officer said gravely: "This is a general announcement to all ranks. I have just received the following message from the military headquarters of our fleet."

Quietly, he read the message.

It is hereby declared that a state of war exists between the peoples of the Fifty Suns and the Earth ship *Star Cluster*. The fleet shall place itself in the path of the enemy and seek battle. Ships incapacitated and in danger of capture must destroy their star maps; and all Meteorological and Astrogation officers aboard such vessels are patriotically required to commit suicide. It is the declared policy of the sovereign government of the Fifty Suns that the invader must be destroyed.

Maltby listened, pale and tense, as Dreenhan went on in a more conversational tone.

I have private information that the government has drawn the conclusion from our experience that the *Star Cluster* released us because they dared not rouse the anger of our people. From this and other data, the leaders have decided that the Earth ship can be destroyed by a determined attack. If we dutifully follow the exact instructions we have received, then even the capture of individual ships will give the enemy no advantage. I have already appointed executioners for all Meteorological and Astrogation officers in the event that they cannot act for themselves at the crucial moment, so please take note.

Captain Peter Maltby, chief meteorologist of the *Atmion*, and an assistant astrogator, noted with a sick awareness that he was committed. He had laid down a policy of united action with the people of the Fifty Suns. It was out of the question that he, for personal reasons, now hastily abandon that attitude.

His only hope was that the wolves of space—as the warships were often called—would by pack action make short work of a single Earth ship.

They ran into a tiger.

VII

She had lost the plebiscite by a heart-breaking nine to ten vote. Grimly, she ordered the big ship to alter course for home.

Late that "day," Communications called her. "Shall we continue to broadcast our course?"

At least she still had control over that. "Most certainly," she said curtly.

The following afternoon, she awakened from a nap to the sound of alarm bells ringing.

"Thousands of ships ahead!" reported Captain Chief of Operations.

"Slow for action!" she commanded. "Battle stations."

When that was done and their speed was less than a thousand miles a second, she spoke to the captains in council.

"Well, sirs and ladies," she said with unconcealed delight, "I should like to have authorization to wage battle against a recalcitrant government, which is now showing that it is capable of taking the most hostile action against Earth civilization."

"Gloria," said one of the women, "please don't rub it in. This is one of your times for being right."

The vote to accept battle was unanimous. Afterward, the question was asked:

"Are we going to destroy them or capture them?"

"Capture."

"All of them?"

"All."

When the Fifty Suns fleet and the Earth ship were some four hundred million miles apart, the *Star Cluster* set up a field that took in a vast section of space.

It was a miniature universe, intensely curved. Ships pursuing an apparently straight course found themselves circling back to their original positions. Attempts to break out of the trap by attaining velocities in excess of light-speed proved futile. A shower of torpedoes directed at the source of the field veered off and had to be exploded in space to avoid damaging their own ships.

It was found impossible to communicate with any planets of the Fifty Suns. Subspace radio was as silent as death.

At the end of about four hours, the *Star Cluster* set up a series of tractor beams. One by one, inexorably, ships were drawn toward the giant battleship.

It was at that time that stern orders were issued for all Fifty Suns Meteorological and Astrogation officers to commit suicide at once.

On the *Atmion* Maltby was one of a pale group of men who shook hands with Vice-admiral Dreehan; and immediately afterward, in the commanding officer's presence, pointed a blaster at the side of his head.

At that penultimate moment he hesitated. "I could take control of him now, this instant—and save my life."

He told himself angrily that the whole affair was futile and unnecessary. Discovery of the Fifty Suns had been inevitable in the sense that it would occur sooner or later, regardless of what he did now.

And then he thought, "This is what I've stood for among the Mixed Men. We must be one with the group, to death, if necessary."

His brief hesitation ended. He touched the activator of his weapon.

As the first captured ships were boarded by teams of technicians, the exultant young woman on the bridge of the greatest ship that had ever entered the Greater Magellanic Cloud learned of the suicides.

Pity touched her. "Revive them all!" she ordered. "There is no need for anyone to die."

"Some of them are pretty badly splattered," was the answer. "They used blasters."

She frowned at that. It meant an immense amount of extra work. "The fools!" she said. "They almost deserve death."

She broke off. "Use extra care! If necessary, put whole ships through the matter transmitter with emphasis on synthesis of damaged tissues and organs."

Far into the sleep period, she sat at her desk receiving reports. Several revived astrogators were brought before her;

and, with the help of Lieutenant Neslor, of Psychology, she questioned them.

Before she retired to sleep, a lost civilization had been found.